I0784448

The author welcomes correspondence at jnaillon@mail.com

If you're reading this, thank you for taking a chance with my humble tale! For my family, I know I can be a chore, so thank you for putting up with me.

In this work, the realm of Southwilde is a melting pot of traditions, legends, and beliefs. Some will seem familiar because various traditions, legends, and beliefs from our world inspired them. Everything in this work is a fictional depiction of Southwilde and their cultural practices, past or present.

CONTENTS

Summer Day

They were a people without the concerns of others, content with their simple, uncluttered way of life. Their quaint village lay beyond the majestic peaks of the Brown Rock Mountains in a vast realm known as Southwilde. For eight generations, the people of South Peak Village enjoyed fertile grounds for farming, lush pastures for their herds, and woods full of game to hunt. As the sun dawned, a girl on the cusp of womanhood strolled the banks of the High Bush River with her father. However, these two were not ordinary denizens of South Peak. He, as a dozen generations before him, was a druid. The young woman who strolled with him, a fledgling druid, hoped to follow the druid path.

"Tell me what you know of change, what it means," he requested.

She paused at her father's curious request and pointed toward the rising sun. "Change is when something becomes different. The world warms when the sun rises."

He stopped to pick up a wilted leaf from the ground and gave it to her. "And this leaf?"

"A change in the season when the leaves wilt and fall from the trees."

"And what of tomorrow?" he asked.

"Our farmers will plant the seeds for the summer harvest," she replied.

"And what other change will happen tomorrow?" he asked.

A grin tugged at the corners of his lips, which prompted a massive eye roll from her. "Father, you would have to be deaf and blind not to know what's happening tomorrow. Mother's planned it since the day I was born."

"That causes me to mention what you didn't say about change."

"Which is... ?" she asked.

"That change is inevitable, such as changing the seasons and birthdays," he said with an affectionate nudge.

"Father, why do we stroll along the river bank this morning, talking of change?"

"I sense change coming... great change," he said pensively.

"So, I'm to call you Seer instead of Druid?"

He continued to speak as if he hadn't heard her comment. "I sense great change, but more than that... an upheaval."

"I don't know what upheaval means, but by the look on your face, I'm not sure I want to know. Is everything well?" she asked and laid a hand on his arm.

He patted her hand. "I don't mean to worry you. Perhaps my thoughts are running amok this morning. Come, let's see what your mother has prepared for breakfast."

***

As the sun rose to greet the first day of summer, Naria exhaled a long-suffering sigh and looked to the heavens for help. She felt poked, prodded, and groomed her to the end of her patience.

"Mother, please, I've had enough! You know how I hate all this fuss!" she pleaded.

"Humor your mother; it's not every day that a girl comes of age in this village. I've dreamed of this since the day you were born."

"Why couldn't I have been born a male? They get to go out and hunt when they come of age! Something useful, something interesting! I must endure a ceremony displaying my... *eligibility,*" she spluttered, "It's embarrassing!"

Leeda placed her hands on her daughter's shoulders to calm her, and there were times she honestly didn't understand her. Her own coming-of-age day was the most memorable of her life, save her marriage day. "It's tradition, an honored tradition at that. You're smart and pretty, so why be embarrassed? There were eight fine young men at the door this morning asking your father for permission to court you! Eight! And it's only morning!" she declared cheerfully.

The hut door swung open, and Nidale placed another suitor's offering on the dining table with a sigh. "Make those nine young men," he said dryly.

"Father, please say that Doonay was one of them! He's the only one I'd even consider!"

"Yes, my falling leaf. He was the first," he assured her. "He tried to scare the others away, but until you've formally declared your intention—"

Naria rolled her eyes. "I know, heaven help me, that anyone can seek my hand until I declare my intention. Don't they know that Doonay and I have been friends since we could walk?"

"Childhood friends are one thing; a potential wife is another. Not only are you of age today, but you're the future druid of this village. I imagine there will be a minor war among the men for your hand," her father teased.

"Hanya only had three suitors," her mother added smugly.

"Mother, she's my friend. Be nice!" Naria chided. "My being a druid, that's not known. Not until I complete the vision quest, if I receive a vision at all."

Her father placed his hands on her shoulders and peered into her eyes as he spoke. "It's known among our people that only druids have green eyes. There are only two pairs of green eyes in this village, and they belong to us. When you were a child, the others made mud cakes while you made poultices. You sensed your grandfather's spirit, and it didn't scare you. You're Druid, I'm certain of it."

While Naria finished her ritual preparations, Nidale appraised his daughter once more. It might be the thoughts of a proud father, but she was the prize of the village, he was sure of it. Whatever young man would catch her pretty eyes wouldn't know what hit him.

***

When the sun was at its highest point in the midday sky, Naria began the symbolic rituals of her coming-of-age ceremony. The entire village gathered at the lodge of the celebrant. She emerged, clad a new woman's doe-skin tunic, and placed her belongings outside the door.

South Peak's chief elder spoke. "Nidale, do you present your daughter as a woman of our people on this day?"

"I do."

The elder nodded and turned to Naria. "Are you ready to take your place as a woman of our people?"

"I am ready, elder."

Her mother joyfully raised her hands to the sky.

"Are your food and crafts prepared for the feast?"

"It is, elder."

The feast the elder spoke of was another part of the ritual. Naria had spent most of her time preparing food and various crafts for the feast days before the ceremony. Potential suitors sampled her culinary offerings and evaluated her skills to judge her suitability as a homemaker for her future family. Her parents stood proudly behind her as she warmly greeted everyone who stepped forward and sampled her venison stew, which was a success. Feasting, dancing, storytelling, and games of chance and skill lasted well into the night. Children gathered around a fire to listen to Naria play songs on her wooden flute. She bid the children goodnight and brought the flute to her lips. Before she played another note, hands came from behind and covered her eyes.

"Will it be Naria's bedtime soon?" a masculine voice playfully asked.

She pretended to yawn and face Doonay, who pulled her to her feet and nodded toward the High Bush River. Several men standing nearby that waited to talk to her shook their heads and mumbled as Doonay led her to the river. They walked silently along the riverbank, neither one knowing what to say. She realized that the feelings of their friendship had subtly shifted. Did her friend now look at her as a potential wife? How would things change between them? Doonay broke the awkward silence when he nervously cleared his throat.

"It's a pleasant night out," he remarked.

"It's the solstice; the moon is at its fullest," she replied.

"I... I shouldn't be having this much trouble."

"What trouble?"

"Talking to you, falling leaf."

Her exasperation level rose once more. "It's just me, Naria, the girl you've known your whole life... and I wish people would stop calling me that!"

When she was seven, she climbed a moon fruit tree to get the last of the season's unpicked fruit and fell from the limb. She broke her arm, and since that day, her nickname had been "falling leaf."

"As of today, you're not a girl... now wait, that wasn't right..." he stammered and frowned at his jumbled words.

"Ah, I see. Father said you were one of my suitors this morning."

He ran a hand through his hair, straightened his tunic collar, and cleared his throat before speaking. "I know you're leaving for your quest tomorrow, but when you return, w-would you consider letting m-me court you?"

She had never seen her friend so out of sorts, so she laid her hand on his arm to calm him. "Like I told Father this morning, you're the only one I'd ever consider."

"I saw you talking to Sondow, and he likes you, so—"

Sondow likes me? She held up her hand to halt his worried rambling. "I had to play a part today, and I had to talk to everyone. Sondow was admiring the fishing net I wove, which your father taught me to make years ago."

His smile glowed in the moonlight when he removed the bear tooth necklace he was wearing and held it out to her. "I want you to have it."

"I can't take it; it's from your hunt the day you came of age!"

"Please wear it. I know it's not what you deserve, but it would mean much to me if you would wear it."

"All right, if it means much to you, I will."

After he put it around her neck, they shared their first kiss.

Going West

The following day, Nidale stood beside his daughter and looked at the western horizon just after dawn. Her mother looked on with worried, tearful eyes.

"So today is my falling leaf's day," Nidale said softly, his voice wavering.

"Yes, father," Naria replied solemnly.

It was the day the fledgling had been waiting for her entire life. It was finally the time for her to set out on her vision quest. Fledglings could not travel the Druid path without their first visions seared to their mind. Her father explained that the searing would happen literally. If she were a druid, the magic in her blood would boil, and she would be feverish near death upon seeing the visions. If she survived, she would return home a druid. She couldn't bear to think of the alternative, to return as a mundane woman in the village, destined to cook and clean her whole life. In her heart of hearts, she knew that her destiny held more. For as long as she could remember, she trained and dreamed to become a druid worthy of her people. She did her best to learn her father's knowledge and skills, and when his spirit passed on, she would be the druid of her people. She looked down at her woman's tunic given to her the previous day and wondered if she was truly ready. She stood on the village's outskirts with only her sturdy oak staff and looked to the west.

The people gathered to see the start of her journey. Doonay gazed affectionately at her, the memory of last night's kiss still fresh in his mind. He was proud of her, but it mingled with concern over her well-being while on her quest. When he first learned of it, he couldn't believe his ears.

"Nidale, what kind of mad quest requires a young woman to venture alone in the wilderness, for who knows how long, with only a stick? No water, no food, no shelter, no bow? Most men would have trouble with this! How will she survive?"

When she returned from the quest, he would ask her father for her hand in marriage. He was sure Naria would accept. After all, he was the village's best hunter, and his father often said he would be an Elder, so who else would she choose? Sondow, the bowl maker? Surely not. He had seen her with no one else, so he supposed she wanted only him.

"... and as the telling stones have said, you must make your way west until the sun sets. Meditate and ponder your life's meaning where you finally stop. Consider every element of the world, every creature around you, and the part that both play. Take nothing but this staff and return only with it and your visions. Safe journey, daughter," Nidale said, and his voice again wavered.

"Doonay, you may come and bid goodbye to your beloved," he said over his shoulder, rolling his eyes.

"Father, he means well," Naria scolded.

"I know, I'm teasing."

Doonay snickering older brothers shoved him forward. He straightened himself and kissed her as a betrothed man would, then turned to start her journey. She looked back one last time to see her father and mother waving. Doonay put his hand over his heart as a heartfelt farewell gesture in the way of the people. She returned the gesture and, with a deep breath, turned toward her destiny.

***

Hours later, Naria peered at the sky and glared at the unrelenting midday sun. Lamentably, she foraged for anything edible to calm her rumbling stomach, but she could think of nothing apart from the delicious venison steaks the night before. *Just think of how hungry I'll be tonight... no! I'm not here to eat; I seek my vision!*

As the sweltering hours passed, she wondered if her father had endured such a trial on his vision quest. She had never known such heat, such thirst! Irritated, she swore when she stumbled and snagged her tunic on a bush, and then cheered when she discovered the bush bore edible berries. When the sun finally set, she felt like she had walked for days. She came upon a stream and followed it into a thicket, grateful for the shade of the trees. She was famished, but exhaustion overpowered the needs of her stomach, and she lay down on the ground. *I'll ponder the world around me when I can keep my eyes open long enough to ponder.*

Startled into awareness, she woke to the feel of damp earth and moisture on her face. *I don't even remember falling asleep!* She saw that it was early morning, and during her slumber, it had rained. Her body ached from the arduous trek and night on the hard ground. A loud, melodic growl from her belly proclaimed it was time for food. She wished to take her mind off her hunger, but she could think of nothing else. Feeling lonelier than ever, desperately hungry, and more skeptical about herself than ever before was part of a more important lesson. She had to endure the trial independently, relying on her wits, skills, and the world around her. First things first, as her father often said. Knowing that she needed something more substantial than roots and berries to sustain her, she set out to craft a simple fishing net or a snare for a small animal. As she searched the thicket for the materiel, she was delighted to find vines of gourds. She could use the rinds as bowls, eat their fruit, and fashion the vines for rope. She walked along the stream bed and found shells with sharp edges that would be useful as cutting tools.

When the sun was high in the midday sky, she ate berries, roots, and gourds as the net and snare had caught nothing. She cut her hand when she sliced a gourd and counted many insect bites, so she set out to forage the ingredients for a medicinal salve. As she applied the salve, her mind wandered to when her father had teased her about her salves. How much she missed him! She was sure he was the wisest druid ever, and his courage was without question. He often faced the awful illnesses and injuries of others without question and stood with the village elders against the rivals and malcontents of their people. Her thoughts turned to Doonay. Was he the man of her heart? Were his kisses the answer to her question? She recalled how his kiss made her feel flushed all over, and a warm feeling lingered in her belly. *What do I think if that's just from a kiss, heavens above? This heat and hunger are affecting my mind.*

Her reverie was interrupted when she saw a silvery flash from the stream, that prompted her to snatch the net from the water. It wasn't a big fish, but there would be more than berries for supper. Her mouth watered as she roasted the fish and happily ate her excellent supper with the promise of better sleep that night with a full belly.

***

Nidale, just like his daughter, startled into awareness back at South Peak, but for a different reason. He'd had a frightening dream of his village being attacked by people he had never seen. As a young druid, he'd traveled much of the continent, but the attackers were people unknown to him. *Who would attack us? Why? We're not a threat to anyone.*

He shuddered as he recalled the dream. The village's homes were ransacked and destroyed. The frightened people crying and angry while forced away from their burning homes, with swords at their backs. To what purpose was such an awful vision? It was a warning from the spirits; he was sure of it. Sometimes it took him days to arrive at the purpose of a dream, but not this one, and it was terrifying and unmistakable. The critical question remained: when would this terrible event occur? He needed to meditate and ask the spirit of Destiny to help him solve the dream's dilemma.

Leeda saw the troubled look on her husband's face as he gathered incense and telling stones. His hands trembled as he placed the objects in a pouch, so she couldn't imagine what sort of vision would cause fear in the bravest man she knew.

"My heart, is there anything I can do?"

He let out his breath and slung the satchel over his shoulder. "I don't mean to worry you, but there is something you can do. Get some things together, not much, just what you need. We may need to leave in a hurry."

Of course, now she was worried. "Leave? Hurry? When?"

"I'm not sure; that's what I'm going to find out."

He kissed her quickly, left their lodge, and walked about the village. As he greeted those going about their morning, he asked himself over and over, who would attack these peaceful people? They had no enemies, as far as he knew. The nearest neighboring people inhabited a village a day's journey to the south, and South Peak enjoyed civil relations with them. For eight generations, the people of South Peak farmed, fished, and hunted. They were potters, wood-shapers, and tailors, not people who warred for wealth and power. The South Peak hunters were among the best on the continent, but they weren't warriors. To shoot an arrow at a deer was one thing; to shoot an arrow at a person was altogether different concept.

He left the village's confines and crossed the High Bush river bridge, where he arrived at a grove shaded by dozens of enormous oak trees, the tallest on the continent. Two shorter ones marked the people's burial grounds entrance, while the tallest marked where he would meditate, Tall Oak Den. He moved aside brush and uncovered the door to the den used for prayer and meditation. Inside, he lit the incense, arranged the telling stones, and prayed for clarity and strength.

The Meditations

Half a day's distance away, Naria prayed for the same. She felt agitated and ill without knowing why. *Is this part of gaining a druid's spirit, or did I eat a bunch of spoiled berries?* Her head ached, she felt fevered, and her heart pounded. *I must get control of myself!* She sat down, leaned against a tree, and let her hands rest on the ground. She closed her eyes and recalled her father's words. *Ponder life's meaning where you stop. Consider every element of the world, every creature around you, and the part they play.*

She inhaled and took in the unique scent of the tree at her back. She felt the soft, damp earth on her hands and inhaled the smell of the soil. *That's odd; I've never noticed that dirt had a particular aroma.* She felt sleepy, with no need to move from her spot, and smiled when a cool breeze drifted through the thicket. A crack of thunder brought her out of her meditation, and she lifted her face to the sky to let the deluge douse her grimy, fevered body. The rain had never felt so good. She greeted it like a long-lost friend, grateful for the relief it brought, and wondered how long it would stay. Feeling light as air, her vision faded until she saw no more, and her body slumped to the ground.

Once again she woke, but this time to a completely unfamiliar sensation. She was curious and frightened when she saw her sleeping form in the dark of night. She looked closer and saw the rise and fall of her chest. *No, not dead, needed to be sure!* She lifted her hand and saw that it was translucent. She nudged her body with her foot, but it passed through her thigh, causing her physical body to shudder. She passed her translucent hand in front of her face and the motion brought on a moment of panic. *Is this my spirit? What do I do now? How do I get back into my body?! Father said nothing of this!*

She turned and looked at the thicket, amazed at what she saw. The trees and stream gave off a faint glow, while the light of the animals scurrying about was brighter and solid. Auras! She looked at her body and noted her aura was more substantial than anything else in the thicket. She felt like she was falling and woke with a gasp back in her body. Unbearably thirsty, she crawled to the stream, weak again from hunger and a never-ending fever. She cupped the water to drink, splashed it on her face, and prayed for fortitude to endure the rest of her quest. Like an answer to a prayer, a snared fish splashed in the stream.

***

Nidale meditated most of the day and into the night and had seen little that would be of use. When he was about to give up and leave the den, he became transfixed by a vision of his daughter. She sprawled on the ground and gasped for breath as her hands dug into the soil. She gasped, "Father, it burns!" with a muted scream through clenched teeth. He grimaced in sympathy for her, knowing first-hand the agony she would experience as the Druid power seared itself in her blood. There was no telling what visions she would see; every fledgling had unique dreams tailored just for them.

He slumped to the ground when his own visions began. He saw the early morning sunrise and the renegade's horses, marked differently from South Peak's horses. He next saw his wife knock a bowl of breakfast porridge from the dining table and irritably throw a rag on the kitchen countertop. The third sequence featured a group of the invaders jeering as they stomped through the fields of newly planted crops. The early morning chill in the den brought him back to the present. He had a clue, at least; he was sure of it. For that, he was grateful, but the question remained: what morning would the invaders arrive? He left the den, went to the fields, and noted that the shoots looked like those in his vision. He hurried to his lodge and entered. Inside, he saw Leeda knock a bowl of breakfast porridge off the table and throw the rag, irritated, just as he had seen in his dream. As soon as he arrived, he left.

"You don't doubt this, Nidale?" the chief elder queried.

"I wouldn't stand before you otherwise, and I've never given you a reason to doubt my visions. The attack could be as soon as tomorrow morning."

"What can we do? If this terrible thing happens, what chance do we have?" an elder asked. "There are no defenses or warriors here, only hunters who have hunted only game, and not enough to fight off an attack," the chief elder stated.

"There are also over two dozen pregnant women, many children, and the old and sickly who can't move as quickly as we need," another elder added.

"To make us seem less of a threat, send our best young hunters away," Nidale suggested as he thought of the hot-headed Doonay. "Better yet, send a woodworker with them on the pretense of inspecting trees or some similar task."

"Are you thinking clearly about such a plan?" an elder scoffed.

"They'll be hard-pressed to leave, knowing what's to happen. We know our young men; they would rather fight and die than run away like cowards," another elder declared.

Nidale took a deep breath and spoke. "Then we won't tell them," he insisted and held his hands up to stop the protest. "I hate to lie, but in this case, we must. This isn't the time to worry about how we look; this is about saving our people's lives! Once the party has left, we can tell our people and plan our survival as best we can."

"Your daughter is west, is she not?" the chief elder questioned.

Nidale nodded. "She is."

"Is there a chance the party might meet with your daughter?"

"A chance, yes."

"Who is to leave?" another elder asked.

"I urge you to consider Doonay, Aldren, and the spear twins. They have no wives or children. I would think the woodworker Tholan is the best choice from the craftsmen to make the ruse complete."

"So, it comes to this uncertain plan? We spare our best young hunters, a woodworker, and a fledgling druid so that our people will not be lost. May fate be with us," the chief elder intoned sadly.

"They will remain safe and free to seek help. We can only hope they come to realize it," Nidale maintained.

He returned home to break the news to his wife as best he could. How could he break the news to his wife that their village would be destroyed, and they might never see their daughter again? He entered his home and took his wife's hands into his.

"My heart, what I'm about to tell you will be hard to hear."

***

After breakfast, the chief elder spoke to the assembled hunters, Doonay among them. "We look to expand the borders of our village to the west. I've called our best hunters to accompany Elder Danarin to judge the land's suitability. Tholan will also make the journey to judge the quality of the wood from the trees. Our Druid told us of a vision of an unusual herd of elk, so it will be more than a sight-seeing trip."

"What do you mean when you say *unusual*?" Doonay inquired.

"In my dream, these elk were the largest and fastest I've ever seen," Nidale replied and resisted the urge to roll his eyes at the absurdity of the tale.

"Pashah! That means nothing to a strong bow and fast arrow!" Doonay declared.

"You leave in an hour. Good fortune to you all," the chief elder said.

The elders unanimously chose Danarin, the youngest elder at forty-seven, to join the young men.

"Brothers, I am heartsick to leave you. To lead these young ones away under a lie makes it even worse."

"You're the best choice, Danarin. You have no wife or children to worry about, and you'll be able to withstand the journey far better than the rest of us. The young men will need your guidance," the chief elder stated.

Danarin prepared his pack and thought of the young men who would unknowingly flee the village. Despite their youth, Doonay and Aldren earned the reputation of being masters of the hunt. One would think that the bold and hot-headed personality of Doonay would clash with Aldren's easy-going, humorous nature, but the two friends were as close as brothers. No one was more skilled than Beldos and Valdos with spears in hand. They anticipated and echoed each other's thoughts and actions as only twins could do, that made them a valued asset on any hunt. He emerged from his lodge and saw the woodsman Tholan choose his tools for the journey. The young artisan contemplated a hatchet in his hand and threw it at a plank of wood twenty paces away. It landed dead center, and a group of children nearby cheered and ask him to do it again. He wondered what the parents of the others would say if they knew what was to happen, and paused in remembrance of Nidale's pleading request when they spoke earlier.

"Danarin, I know that it's much to ask, considering what is to happen, but I wish to ask... no, to beg something of you. If you should happen across my daughter, please look after her as if she were your own. I can't bear the thought of my Naria out there with no one to look after her.

She's a young woman soon to be without her parents and a fledgling druid without a guide."

"I will look after her; you have my word on that. I once had a daughter, so I know how precious she is to you," Danarin assured him.

"I must urge that if you come across Naria during her burning, you'll want to help her, but you mustn't approach her. She'll be in agony, but she must endure it; she knows this. The magic is deadly to those who aren't Druid," Nidale explained.

THE INVASION

The following day, the invaders were ready for battle when they entered South Peak village just after sunrise. They didn't expect to meet three hundred villagers waiting for their arrival. In front of the galloping throng, the invaders' leader held his sword high to signal them to stop. *What trickery is this?* He saw a man dressed differently than the others wielding a staff and holding a woman close. *Their leader, I assume. Very well, we will see what this leader has to say.*

"Ten of you follow me. The rest of you stay back until you're called!"

He didn't specify which ten, but ten armed men nodded at each other and slid from their horses to join him. He stopped at Nidale, pointed his sword at him and waited for a reaction. He noted the simple tunic and unusually bright green eyes of the angrily silent man, who didn't even glance at the sword.

"I am Commander Lanard. Are you the leader of this village?"

His eyes never left Lanard's. "I am not," he replied evenly.

The chief elder stepped forward and spoke. "I am the chief elder of South Peak village."

With a parting glance at Nidale, he walked to the elder and sheathed his sword.

"Where are the warriors of this village?"

"We have no warriors."

"How can that be? Look at the size of your men!" he exclaimed incredulously.

"We don't need warriors. What purpose would they serve peaceful people? We don't make senseless war upon others to assert our power... or take what isn't ours."

The commander felt a subtle insult at the elder's answer and looked at the people, where defiance was tinged with sadness. "Brave but foolish words from the leader of a defenseless people," he sneered to bait the elder.

"You asked, I answered."

The commander stepped closer and spoke. "I have killed men for lesser words."

The elder shrugged. "I've no fear of death. I'm 76 seasons old; death comes closer every day. We're old friends."

The commander narrowed his eyes, turned on his heel, and stalked back to the ten men waiting for orders. "Take twenty men and search the village. Report back to me in an hour."

The men brought their fists to their chests and trotted off. An hour later, they stood around the commander with assorted belongings of the village.

"This is it?" he growled.

He frowned at pottery, carved wood, animal skins, cooking utensils, and food. Behind him, two of his men whispered over a couple of smaller leather pouches.

"You there! What do you hold, and why haven't you shown it?" he demanded.

"N-no excuse, commander," one warrior stammered and held out the pouch.

Lanard snatched it from the man's hand and emptied it on the ground, and what he saw took his breath away. Brightly colored gems, prized for their worth in every corner of the continent, lay scattered at his feet.

"Is this the only bag?" he asked with an amazed whisper.

"No, commander, there's more," another said and held up a second pouch.

He picked up a green gem between his forefinger and thumb to examine it in the sunlight. "It appears there is value here, after all."

***

The commander had the elders brought to a commandeered lodge and demanded they explain the gems' presence.

"Our crafters work them into their creations, such as that adorned bowl next to your foot. They hold a different value to us," the chief elder explained.

"You could buy an army with these gems," he said and nudged a crate filled with pouches of gems.

"We trade everything we need or want among ourselves. We do not need money, nor would any of us think to ask for a price for the necessities of life. We've lived this way for eight generations. Your ways do not interest us."

Again, the commander felt a subtle insult at the elder's words. "The governor of this province will be interested in your ways. Your people could be powerful and wealthy, yet you have no interest in things of the world."

There was a commotion outside of the hut and the voice of someone praying for patience. A guard stepped inside and raised a fist against his chest.

"Commander, the tall, strange one wants to talk to you."

Lanard sighed. "All of them are tall.... let him in."

Nidale stepped in and gave the chief elder an are you well look. The chief nodded quickly.

"Speak; I want to leave before nightfall. The hill cats get feisty after dark," Lanard drawled.

"One of our old ones has been ill, I need to treat him."

"Are you a healer?"

"No."

"Then what is your purpose?"

"Healing is one of my duties. I am Druid."

Several guards in the hut gasped and a guard outside cursed.

"Calm yourselves!" Lanard barked.

He didn't believe in superstitions and religious nonsense, but many of his men did. Word would pass quickly of the Druid's presence. He had faced this kind of thing before and could never comprehend the appeal of religion or the influence that one person's presence could have on a situation. He had to reassure his men that he had control and that they wouldn't be cursed to the four winds.

"Come, Druid, walk with me and show me your healing ways. No guards will join us so you can perform your duties without distraction."

The warriors watched as their commander observed the Druid care for a sickly older man. "What ails him?"

"He has a breathing sickness and fevers."

"Can anything be done?"

"No. The most I can do is see that the passing is painless."

"When will that be?"

"His spirit decides the time, but I guess it won't be much longer. His wife and sons have already passed; he longs to join them."

The wait wasn't long, two hours at the most. The man's spirit decided that he had been there long enough. There was no more he could teach the younger ones in such a weakened condition, and it looked as if his village and people would be no more. He muttered a thank you to Nidale and fell asleep, never to wake.

"I will allow you to perform whatever your people do at these times. We burn our dead and release the ashes to the wind," Lanard said.

"We return our dead to the earth, offer prayers for the grieving who knew him, and thank the spirit for sharing their life with us."

"Do what you must quickly, Druid; we leave before nightfall."

***

Naria didn't know if it was day or night in the thicket, nor did she care. All she knew was the burning pain that surged through her body. She lay on the ground, clutching the dirt, screaming through clenched teeth. The ground rumbled, but she didn't notice. The burning sensation subsided for the time being, and in her mind, she saw her mother knock a bowl from the dining table. She then she saw her father talking to strange men with a sword at his back. She uselessly reached for him and arched her back as more burning pain wracked her body.

"Father, it burns!" she screeched when a vision of her village burning to the ground settled in her mind. So vivid was the image that she could smell the smoke and feel the flame's heat, then the visions then shifted to curious sights.

She saw herself surrounded by children as she tossed a net into a lake.... feeding an elppa to a black pony with a white spot on its chest... talking and laughing with a young man sporting fair-colored hair... gazing in wonder at the tall, white stone walls.

The burning pain waned, and she drifted into welcome unconsciousness.

Becoming

"Just where are these wondrous elk?" Doonay asked dryly. "We've wandered around here all day!"

"They probably heard you whine and went the other way," Beldos chided.

"Or they got a whiff of you, Aldren," who sniffed under his arm.

"Elder, what say you?" Doonay asked.

Danarin heard him ask a question but concentrated on a set of small footprints leading into a thicket.

"That's surely not the prints of an elk unless it wears wee shoes," Doonay commented.

"Could a child or woman of the village have wandered off this far?" Tholan asked.

"I can only think of one," Doonay stated, an anxious edge to his voice.

They followed the footprints along a stream into a thicket. Across the stream, they noticed a familiar oak staff on the ground. Aldren called out and pointed to a familiar figure curled up on the ground.

"Naria!" Doonay shouted and started across the stream, but Danarin grabbed his arm.

"No, Doonay, you mustn't!" he urged.

Doonay shook his arm off. "She could be hurt or sick!"

"I know how much you want to go to her, but you mustn't!"

"What are you not telling me, elder?"

"Her father warned me before we left the village that we might come across her. She's taking on Druid magic; contact with her will be deadly to you."

"She would never hurt me!"

"I know that, but from what her father told me, she isn't aware of what's happening outside her mind. Her magic will kill you, and she wouldn't even know it."

"But it looks like a storm is coming, and creatures roam these woods at night! It's called Wolf Woods for a reason! How can I stand by and watch?!"

"She knows she must endure this! We can keep the creatures away, but anything beyond that—"

"We must stand by and watch," Doonay spat and watched the sun set to the longest night of his life.

He could do nothing but watch Naria writhe on the ground, crying in agony. When sobbed and flailed her arms as if fending off an attacker, it took three of them to hold him back. Suddenly, the fight in her mind stopped. She fell still and sat up. She slowly stood, swayed, and lifted her arms. Her eyes opened, startling the group.

"Look!"

"Her eyes glow!"

She chanted words unknown to them and shouted exultant praises to whatever spirits listened. A strong wind blew into the thicket and swirled about her. There she stood; eyes glowing as she proudly called forth the winds as a companion for the night. They had seen nothing so magnificent. The wind seemed playful as it swirled about her, ducked under bushes, and whirled around the trees. It left as quickly as it came, and as if to give her a gift in parting, flower petals drifted down to rest on her head and shoulders. The group had no words for what they witnessed. She fell to her knees, took deep, cleansing breaths, and dug her hands into the soil. Again, she chanted words known only to her, and the surrounding earth trembled. Doonay felt the tree next to him shudder, and something hit the top of his head. He looked down to see that an acorn had fallen from the tree. She eased to a sitting position on the ground and closed her eyes, clutching fistfuls of dirt. They thought she might have fallen asleep until she lifted her arms to the sky again. There was a crack of thunder above them, then rainfall. Doonay now understood what she had described in their previous conversations. She summoned the wind, urged the ground to move, and now called water from the sky. The remaining element was fire. Lightning flashed from the sky, and she turned her glowing eyes to the sight. She cocked her head to one side as if she listened to something and held out her hand. A ball of fire flared into existence in her palm.

"The spirits are truly with her!" Beldos whispered.

She looked at the remains of a campfire and tossed the fireball on top of the kindling. Despite the rain, the fire flourished. They waited in breathless anticipation for the next display of power. They saw her collapse to the ground instead, and she didn't move the rest of the night.

***

The men woke the following day, splashed water on their faces, and ate their remaining nuts and honey cakes.

"I'm indeed hungry; we hunt today," Doonay stated and the others nodded in agreement.

Coughs and mumbling from the other side of the stream drew their attention.

Naria woke disoriented, face down in the dirt. *Why am I on the ground again?* She spat the dirt from her mouth and wiped it from her lips. Parched, she looked for the closest water source, a gourd she had first used to set up camp. Lacking the energy to walk, she crawled to the gourd, and wondered why everything was scattered. When she found the gourd empty, she huffed in frustration and crawled toward the stream.

The men watched her crawl toward the stream. She only had to say the word, and any of them would have fetched her water before the word left her mouth, but apparently, she hadn't realized they were there. She pushed herself to her knees at the stream, cupped her hands in the water, and drank deeply. Deciding that the water would feel marvelous on her grimy and aching body, she crawled into the water and submerged herself completely. Maybe it was her newfound affinity for the elements, but she was certain that she had never experienced a bath quite like this. With a burst of energy, she joyfully played in the invigorating water. She saw what remained of the fishing net and looked around the camp again. It looked like a storm had hit. In the following moments, she remembered the miraculous events of the previous night. Indeed, a storm had hit. She smiled and lifted her arms to the heavens with joy. *I am Druid!*

"Naria?"

Arms raised, she remained still as the the cool water flowed around her body. Only her eyes scanned the area. *Am I still dreaming? Is a spirit talking to me?*

"Naria, it's Doonay."

She slowly turned and saw Doonay, three other hunters, Tholan, the woodworker, and the elder Danarin. She lowered her arms. *How ridiculous I must look!*

"May we approach?" Danarin asked.

She nodded, so they crossed the stream and cautiously approached her.

"Are you well?" Danarin asked.

"Aside from intolerable hunger, I've never felt better," she replied.

Danarin stepped forward and helped her from the stream, and Doonay held out his food pouch.

"What about you? I can't take your food," she said, knowing of Doonay's enormous appetite.

"I've already eaten. Here, I insist."

She took the pouch. It was only nuts, berries, and two honey cakes, but it was a veritable feast for her. She made quick work of the food, as her hunger took precedence over manners.

"You can have mine as well," Aldren offered chivalrously.

She smiled in gratitude and gobbled down the contents of his pouch.

"Have you seen any elk?" Doonay asked.

She nodded. "When I first arrived here, there was a herd by that pond," she said and pointed north toward a pond in the distance.

"This may be a curious question, but were they large?" he asked.

She chuckled. "Were they large? Doonay, all elk are large to me. They were just elk. I've never had such a peculiar conversation over breakfast!"

Doonay shrugged and tossed a rock into the stream.

"Why in the world are you here? I'm glad to see you, but why are hunters, a woodworker, and an elder having breakfast here with me a day's walk from the village?" she asked.

"Large elk, or so we've been told," Aldren answered with a shrug.

"We sent this party to scout out a possible new settlement to expand the village," Danarin added, perpetuating the lie.

"There were reports of larger-than-life elk in the area," Doonay said dryly.

"And a lush new forest," Tholan added.

"But I think it's been just a wild hanoo chase. There's nothing special about this place at all," Doonay grumbled.

She looked at him incredulously. "Nothing special, you say?"

Doonay knew he might have said the wrong thing, but wasn't sure what it was. "Is this a woman thing?"

Danarin shook his head. *Young men never change.*

She rose to her feet, returned their food pouches, and walked away without a word.

Irritation tinted Tholan's voice when he asked, "Can you think of nothing that would make this place special for her?"

"I don't understand," Doonay said and watched her gather scattered objects around the campsite.

"You've hurt her feelings. She came into her druid powers where you sit, and you declare that there's nothing special about it," Danarin explained.

"I didn't mean to hurt her feelings! Of course, all of this is special; I only meant to say—"

Danarin held up a hand. "If you wish to seek her heart, you must learn to temper your words. You must make your meaning clear without offending, especially with young women."

"I'm not the best with words, but I'll try to do better," Doonay said.

"Or someone else will," Tholan commented.

"Is that a challenge?" Doonay demanded.

"Take it as you will," Tholan answered evenly.

Danarin resisted the urge to roll his eyes. Now was not the time for rivalry over a young woman's affections. Soon, these young people would return to find their homes and families gone, which would be toughest for Naria. He was an Elder, but he was no druid. As a fledgling, she would be without her father's guidance as she grew into her abilities. Unless she came upon another druid, she would be on her own in that respect. He blanched at the thought of a young woman's needs handled best by a mother's guidance. *I'm not a mother either.*

***

The hunters returned with deer and rabbit for supper. Naria discussed village business with Danarin while Tholan examined her oak staff, and the hunters began the business of butchering the game.

"Fine spear you crafted, Tholan. It easily went through this deer's flank," Valdos said.

Tholan nodded to acknowledge the hunter's words and gave Naria back her staff. "That's a splendid piece of wood. No knots, no cracks, and the carvings look like great care's been in their creation."

She nodded. "Father helped me choose the sapling, and we smoothed it for days in the riverbed sand. I chose the carvings myself as the ideas that came to me over the years. I'm not good and've cut my fingers many times."

"Nonsense, this is good work. I can show you a way to avoid hurting your fingers."

"I'd like that very much; I have some new carvings to add now," she replied.

Doonay observed their cozy conversation about a piece of wood, noted its importance to her, and also noted that Tholan the stick man had no trouble talking about it with her. Danarin graciously offered his cloak to Naria to sleep on for the night, and soon they heard her soft snores.

"I've never seen her eat like that," Doonay noted.

"She probably hasn't had a true meal in days," Danarin said.

"It's hard to imagine her coming all this way by herself with nothing but that staff. A strong woman deserves a strong husband," Doonay stated.

"Indeed," Tholan said with a chuckle.

"I'm growing tired of your smart mouth, woodworker," Doonay challenged.

"As I grow tired of your boorish mouth, hunter," Tholan replied sharply.

"Calm yourselves," Danarin urged. "This hostility serves no purpose."

The group heard something scurry through the woods, prompting them to reach for their weapons. A squirrel appeared at the edge of the campsite, unconcerned about their presence, and scampered toward Naria. Amused, they watched it sniff her from head to foot and curl up next to her stomach to settle for the night. The men decided on fire watches to ward away any wolves that might come their way. They were all tired, but Danarin had no desire to sleep. Only he knew there were renegades at their home, and they could be closer to them for all he knew. He wished he could sleep for just a little while, if only to escape the heavy burden he felt in his heart.

Home

The following morning, Danarin stood at the edge of the thicket, looking east. The men stirred to the sound of splashing water, and Naria pulled a fishing net from the stream. The sun peeked over the horizon, a fire was going, and a batch of fish was roasting.

"Breakfast!" she called out happily.

Yawning and stretching, they trudged to the stream to splash water on their faces and wash their hands.

"She's much too cheerful this early morning," Aldren grumbled.

"Come now, here's an excellent breakfast to start the day; we have a long walk ahead of us," she encouraged and laid out roasted fish, sliced gourd flesh, and a tasty mix of nuts and berries.

"I wish there were bread to go along with it," she sighed.

"Never mind that. This is more than we expected," Danarin said. "Your skills do you credit and make your parents proud."

There was no higher compliment for her. "Thank you, elder."

After breakfast, as they made to leave the thicket, Naria spoke. "There is something I must do first. I must thank the spirits for their sustenance and protection, and to leave this place as I found it."

"Very well, we wait," Danarin said.

She was a druid now, so there was no question over the matter. At the edge of the thicket, she placed a hand on a tree and the other gripped her staff. She closed her eyes and silently convened with the elemental spirits. Minutes later, she put her hand over her heart, stepped back, and extended her hand. As a brisk wind swept through the scrub, the ground trembled and took the evidence of their stay into its depths. The squirrel from the previous night scurried down the tree. She stooped and extended her arm, to which the squirrel ran up and settled on her shoulder.

"Now we can leave," she said.

***

Hours later, Aldren spoke. "Naria, you should travel with us more often; your trail food is tasty."

"Women don't go on hunting parties," Doonay commented.

Naria tuned out their discussion and thought of her return home, imagining how pleased and proud her father would be. Within an hour of the village, she experienced another vision of the burning village and frightened people. Startled, she stumbled, and the berries she munched on fell from her hand. Doonay laid his hand on her shoulder.

"Are you heat sick? It's no wonder, traveling in this cursed heat all day," he grumbled and cast an annoyed glance at the sky.

"The closer we come to the village, the more uneasy I feel," she murmured.

The others looked east anxiously. She didn't mean to alarm them, so a feigned moment of feminine weakness might set them at ease again.

"Perhaps you're right about the heat," she said with a shy smile. "May I use your arm from time to time to steady myself?"

"I'll stand on your other side, and you can use my arm too," Tholan offered.

Danarin saw the ploy, unsurprised that her calming actions and manners were that of her father's influence. "We can travel slower; she's not used to such a swift pace on the trail."

"Of course, we weren't thinking," Doonay added.

"You're just in a hurry to get back to your mother's honey cakes," Aldren teased.

She mouthed a silent thank you to Danarin, and they continued. In all honesty, she needed to slow to gather her addled thoughts. After the hour passed, they arrived at the outskirts of the village. A breeze reached them, carrying an unbearably putrid odor.

"Lankash! What a stench!" Aldren exclaimed and slapped his hand over his mouth and nose.

They arrived at the western pastures to a horrific sight. Where the sheep and cattle usually grazed peacefully, dozens were dead and bloated. Flies buzzed around the carcasses, and puddles of congealed blood muddied the brown soil red. They had never seen such carnage, and one twin retched. They looked beyond the pastures to the crops. No farmers tended their fields, no young boys practiced with their bows, and no smoke from cooking fires was seen. There wasn't a soul in sight, and Naria took off at a run.

"Naria, no, come back!!" Danarin called out, and they started after her.

"By the spirits, she's fast," Aldren noted.

She reached the river and fell to her knees when she saw the smoldering remains of the village. She scrambled to her feet and ran across the bridge.

"Mother! Father!" she called.

Maybe they were hiding! Perhaps everyone was hiding from whatever had caused the destruction. She cried out for them in desperation. Where could 300 people hide?

"Mother! Father! Come out! It's Naria!"

It was no use. No one was there. The sudden welling of grief and horror was overwhelming until she felt it from another. Danarin sat on a log and held a child's doll while tears streamed down his face. She recognized the sad knowledge in his eyes. Her heart went out to him for the terrible burden she thought he bore. What would her father do?

"Come, elder, let us talk in the grove," she suggested.

***

In the grove's shade, Danarin revealed the truth.

"You knew, didn't you?" she asked.

She knew her companions would be angry beyond belief. The men looked at her curiously, and Danarin nodded sadly.

"What did you know?" Doonay asked.

"Nidale had a vision of the village destroyed and our people forced from it," Danarin admitted.

The men jumped to their feet, their loud, angry accusations rang throughout the quiet of the deserted village.

"You knew and didn't tell us? Why?!"

"Why would you do such a thing?!"

"They sent us away on a lie while they destroyed our village!"

"We could have done something! Something to stop our people from being led away like cattle!"

"Think of our people, Doonay, *think!* What chance would our people have against an army? Now, look again at this group!" Danarin urged.

"I don't understand!" Doonay exclaimed and flung his hands toward the group. "What does hunting, woodworking, and a woman mean to anything?"

Naria understood. She laid her hand on his arm and spoke. "They sent you away because you would have fought and died."

Doonay shook his head in angry denial.

"You're a fine hunter, but you're not a warrior; none of you are," Danarin stated.

"You were sent away to escape what was to come and find me. Danarin is right when he says to look at this group, because we are the ablest to deal with what lies ahead," she explained, correctly guessing her father's hand in the matter.

"What lies ahead?" Doonay asked.

"We're to seek help for our people," Danarin said. "They aren't dead. Look, there's no blood or bodies on the village grounds."

"Your father is a powerful druid; he could have called down fire to burn the invaders to ash or a flood to wash them away," Valdos said.

She smiled sadly and spoke. "I'm young and I don't mean to lecture, but I learned at my father's knee that using magic for vengeance is like inviting evil through the front door. My power is in my heart, and if I use it for evil, my heart will follow."

"Then what are we to do?" Tholan asked.

"Go after them," Beldos urged.

"The sun is setting. I suggest we gather some food and try to sleep on what's happened. Our thoughts are too troubled to decide anything today," suggested Danarin.

***

After a restless night, Naria said a prayer at sunrise for the safety of her people, wherever they were. She returned from the grove to find four men with sadder faces, if that were even possible.

"What's happened now?" Naria asked.

"The twins have left," Danarin said.

"What do they think to do? Take on an army by themselves?" Tholan asked.

"I understand why they left, and part of me wishes I was with 'em, but our elder is right. We need a plan," Doonay admitted.

"Good, your thoughts are clearer this new day. We need to search through the remains of our homes and gather food and tools for our travels, whatever can be of use. It wouldn't be wise to roam Southwilde empty-handed."

At the charred remains of her home, she worked to push aside the crooked door frame. She felt her father's magic and what she saw surprised her. Inside the home, everything remained undamaged. Discolored and smoked, but not destroyed. Through the cries of surprise from her companions, she knew the others had also made the discovery. Her father had used his powers to protect their belongings from the ravages of the fires. He knew this group would return and need the things! The biggest surprise of all was when she noticed his knapsack. It was sitting there as if he packed it for her with everything she would need for a journey; mortar, pestle, telling stones, candles, and incense were all there. She took up her mother's smaller pack and put things in it too; a sewing kit, a shawl, some cooking implements, and her flute. She noticed combs and hairbands peeking out from under her collapsed bed and put a hand to her hair. It occurred to her she hadn't tended to her hair since she left the village. *What a vain, stupid thing to be worrying about at a time like this!* However, her mother's scolding about hair care throughout her life rang loud and clear in her mind, so she stuffed the combs and hair bands in the bag. Danarin's voice from behind her startled her.

"Have you gathered all that you need?" he asked.

She hitched the sacks on her back. "I think so, but I must go to the den for prayer and meditation."

"Something troubles you?" Danarin asked.

They walked across the bridge toward the shaded grove with pensive expressions.

"I'm not sure about anything right now. While standing in the ruins of my home, I thought about my hair and wondered if combs should be in my pack."

He chuckled. "And are combs in your pack?"

She let out a breath. "Yes, but vanity seems foolish at a time like this."

"It's not so much vanity, but purpose you seek. Your mind is already looking ahead, as are the minds of the others. They're talking about re-building the village, the next hunt, and the joy we'll feel when we see our families again. I'd be worried if you didn't think of things like your hair. You're a druid now, but you're also a young woman with the cares of any other young woman."

"We grieve, but we have to move on," she said, and they stopped in front of the den. "Elder, only a druid may enter," she said apologetically.

"I'll enjoy the grove's shade while you meditate," he said and put his pack on the ground.

The squirrel that adopted her skittered down a nearby tree and sniffed Danarin's pack.

"My furry little friend will enjoy the shade with you," she said.

***

Upon entering the dimly lit den, she immediately dropped to her knees on the bearskin rug. There, she observed the worn area on the rug where her father often sat, a tangible reminder of his presence. She didn't hold back her tears. In this den, there could be no false feelings and hidden emotions. She let out all her despair and anger. She pounded on the ground, imploring Fate, Destiny, or whoever was listening for a sense of understanding. She cried in sadness and confusion until she had no tears left.

Outside, the others joined Danarin in the grove. They settled into an uncomfortable silence at the sound of Naria's cries. Only Tholan seemed to be the least affected.

He shrugged and said, "Women cry."

The others looked at him as if he had spoken in a foreign language.

"Don't look at me like that. I have five sisters, I know this. My little sister has come to me countless times in tears because the eyes fell from her doll's face," he said, smiled sadly.

"What did you do?" Doonay asked. He couldn't imagine what he would do if a little girl came to him crying with a doll in hand.

"I fixed the doll. My father, rest his soul, said that one of our jobs is to keep our women happy. That means fixing whatever problem makes them unhappy. It's harder with my older sisters because a lot of their problems are with men. There's nothing I can do about that."

They laughed.

"We can't fix what's going on in there," Doonay said, nodding toward the den.

The crying and chanting quieted.

"There's nothing we can do. She's a druid and female, so she feels more keenly than we do," Danarin advised.

As night fell upon them, they hunted small game and talked around a fire. Naria emerged from the den with three small bowls, a knife, and a piece of cloth.

"There's one more ritual I must perform before we leave. Please sit with me."

She kneeled on the ground and placed the objects in front of her. "Upon my return, my father would have marked me as Druid, as his father did before him. Sadly, he isn't here, so I must take the task upon myself. It's a privilege for me to sit before you, my people, and take the marks. I pledge to serve our people from now on. I can only hope to live up to the task."

She grasped the knife with her right hand and lifted it to the darkened sky. "I wept in sadness at the loss of our loved ones and the fear they must have felt when forced from their homes with swords at their backs. May we all find happiness again."

She braced herself, cut across her left bicep just below the shoulder, and raised the knife again. "I wept in confusion at the senseless ways of people toward others. May we find reason in the madness."

She made a second cut below the first. A cooling breeze blew through the grove, and she lifted the knife a third time. "I wept in anger at the destruction of our village. May we return with our families to restore our homes."

She made the third cut and laid the knife behind her. She applied the cloth to the cuts until the bleeding stopped and dipped her finger in the bowl that held blue dye.

"I honor the essence of water and air," she stated and swiped the blue shade across the first cut.

"I honor the essence of the good earth," she again stated and used the brown dye on the second cut.

"I honor the essence of fire. As these marks will be with me the rest of my life, so may the essence of each."

She swiped the red dye to the third cut, dug a small hole, and put the bloody cloth in the hole. "This represents the sadness, confusion, and anger that I felt. Join me in putting it to rest."

Five pairs of hands swept dirt over the cloth. "The knife represents pain. I will leave it here so it will cause no more pain, yet I carry the marks it made as a reminder of the pain."

She rose and walked among them as she spoke, and placed her hand over their hearts one by one, as another cool breeze drifted into the grove. "I will leave this place with new spirits guiding me, as I hope you will. Hope, faith, and justice will also be my companions. Can you think of others to join us?"

"Courage," Doonay offered.

"Cleverness," Tholan stated.

"Cheer," Aldren said.

"Worthy companions all," Danarin said.

***

After the marking, Aldren mentioned a sack of vegetables he gleaned from his father's field.

"And with the rabbits, I can make a good stew!" Naria said as she stood to return to the village, then stopped at the bridge and called, "Doonay, come on!"

Doonay grinned and jogged to join her. They returned with her mother's best pot, cooking stone, and a few bags of cooking ingredients. She arranged the pot above the cooking fire and removed a cooking spoon from her pack.

"Naria, this is too much; you don't have to cook for us," Danarin said.

She shrugged. "I'm glad for something to do, and I have the chance to use my mother's prized pot. I don't know if it'll ever be used again, so it makes me happy to use it."

"Your mother doesn't let you use her cooking pot?" Aldren asked.

"Heavens no, she gets nervous when I even look at it. However, what she doesn't know won't hurt me," she said with a wink.

She's just like her father, Danarin mused.

"What's in that bag?" Tholan asked.

"Mix for honey cakes and bread. I gathered as much as I could for the journey."

While the stew simmered, she made the batter for the cakes and checked the cooking stone's heat. She put half a dozen palm-sized cakes on the heated stone to fry. She stirred the stew, sniffed it, and started on the bread dough.

"Can I help?" Tholan offered.

"Of course, you can turn the cakes," she said.

When Naria finished the cake and bread dough, she announced that the stew was ready. Each took a wooden bowl and spoon from their knapsacks and filled their bowls.

After supper, the men thanked her for the meal and left the grove to bathe. From a tree, the squirrel skittered down to eat the honey cake she held out.

"It's just us for now," she said.

***

When the men returned from their baths, they found a stack of honey cakes next to their knapsacks. In the den, Naria arranged her bedroll and prepared for her bath. The men settled in their bedrolls outside the den, talked about which direction to go the next day, and asked the spirits to comfort their loved ones. She returned to her home and rummaged through the debris for cloth and soap. She went to the section of the river where women bathed and stripped out of her dirty tunic and breeches. Cold water was no longer annoying, but a refreshing relief after the day's oppressive heat. Soap in hand, she washed the grime from her body and hair.

Doonay turned on his side in the grove and pulled his blanket to his shoulders. He heard splashing water and opened his eyes. The brush and rocks in his view were parted just enough for a perfect vista of Naria bathing. He knew he should look away, but the scene was mesmerizing. He had never seen a nude woman before. Her back was to him, and she crouched to wash her hair. She stood and flipped her wet hair down her back. When she raised her arms to stretch, the sight of her was almost his undoing. She was breathtaking. The smooth skin of her slender body glistened in the moonlight, and he nearly groaned out loud when she ran her fingertips down her neck and sides. When she massaged the small of her back, she let her head fall back with a muted moan. If she turned around, it would be his happy death; he was sure of it. She moved to the riverbank and started washing her clothes. She muttered to the squirrel sitting nearby and splashed water at it. It responded with chirping and frantic flicking of the tail. Her gentle laugh brought a much-needed smile to Doonay's face.

Going South

When the men woke at sunrise, they found Naria had woke before them again.

"We must seem like a bunch of lazy slugs to her," Aldren said.

"What the devil is she doing?" Doonay asked, peering beyond the wheat fields.

She walked through the tall grass, stooped over occasionally, and put something in a bag.

"Might be some ritual," Aldren suggested.

She stopped, looked at the group, and Doonay waved. She waved back and returned to them.

"Another ritual?" Danarin asked.

She shook her head and held up the bag. "Wild hanoo eggs!"

"What did I tell you? Isn't she the best trail companion ever?" Aldren asked.

During breakfast, Tholan asked a question. "Naria, except for hunting, you have as much skill as any man here. How did this come about?"

She took a drink of water and answered. "When I was born, my father was sure I would be a druid. From the time I could walk, he instructed me in field craft and woods lore. He knew I would need these skills when I left home to explore the world, as all druids do."

"He taught you well," Aldren praised.

"It wasn't only my father. My uncle showed me how to make simple snares, and Doonay's father taught me to make his clever fishing nets. I'm sure that there's something that each of you can teach me. Our chief elder even revealed his secret recipe for trail mix."

"That sounds just like him," Danarin added.

"However, you will discover things about me that will make you scratch your head in wonder about my supposed trail skills. I'm clumsy, terrified of snakes, and hate being dirty, which amuses my father to no end."

***

After breakfast, staff in hand, she stood with the men and readied to leave the only place she'd ever known. They were trying to decide on the direction of travel, which was admittedly tricky because they had no idea where their people were taken.

"The tracks are all over the village, go in no certain direction, and then disappear! I can't track that!" Doonay groused and kicked up dirt in frustration.

Naria sensed her father's energy that erased anything showing their direction, because he knew they would try to follow.

"I say we head to the town south of here, called Baranos. It's known to me. Maybe someone there saw or got word of the force that invaded here. With any luck, they noted the three hundred unarmed men, women, and children with swords at their backs," Danarin stated.

He took smaller pouches of gems from his knapsack and gave a couple to each of them. Doonay took out a red one and held it up in the light, making red beams of light dance on the ground.

"These gems hold little value for us beyond decoration and crafting, but the value is immeasurable for others. The gem Doonay is playing with will buy a hundred horses in the town we're headed to," Danarin explained.

"Lankash!" Aldren exclaimed.

"Aldren, there is a young woman present," Danarin admonished.

"Sorry," Aldren said sheepishly.

"Naria, excuse us," Danarin said and ushered the young men a distance away from the grove to speak. "As an elder of our people, I feel the need to guide you as your fathers would. Do you agree with me on this?"

They all nodded solemnly, so he continued. "I want to remind you of your upbringing, even in this hard time. You've been raised to show proper courtesy for others, a mark of a man of worth. We're simple plains people, but we're not a pack of barbarians. Take a good look at that young woman over there."

They looked at Naria, who casually twirled her staff while she cast surreptitious glances at them.

"Until we know our people's fate, I see Naria as the last remaining female of our people. She should be protected for her abilities and potential."

"We understand, elder."

When Danarin walked away, Doonay gave Aldren a quick slap to the back of the head.

"Is something the matter?" she asked when Danarin joined her.

"No, just some man-to-man talk."

"I see."

"As an elder of our people, I'll try to guide you much as your parents would. However, since you are a young woman alone among men, this task is..."

"Harder?" she offered.

"Yes, but you're not a burden. As an elder, it's my duty. You're Druid, and one day you'll make some lucky man a fine wife. Until we know the fate of our people, I see you as the last woman of our people."

"I understand... I think," she said.

"They must seem like chest-thumping ruffians, but I ask you to be understanding. They're young but trying their best during this hard time."

She placed her hand over her heart. "Elder, I thank you for your wise words. I'm sure my father would be grateful to you to act in his stead."

***

After they filled their water skins, the journey south began. Along the way, they searched for signs of their people, but talk was unnecessary as each person was lost in thought. When the sun was at its highest point, they stopped to eat in the shade of a thicket.

"Danarin, tell us about this town we're headed to; you've been there, haven't you?" Tholan asked.

"Yes, two years ago. Baranos is like nothing you've ever seen. Thousands of people live and work there. Hundreds more that make their living off the town live in nearby villages like our own. The entire town is stone, with no thatch roofs in sight. Money is the driving force of their lives, and the level of greed will probably surprise you, so guard your gems carefully. Some will have no hesitation to take them from you by force."

He let those words of caution settle.

"However, the criminal element is few compared to the entire population, thanks to the town guard. Don't worry if you see armed men roaming the streets; they're part of the town guard. They work to keep it safe."

He turned his attention to Naria. "I know what might interest you. The town has a multitude of faiths and they revere different gods. You might see priests, wizards, and maybe even another druid."

"Wizards?" she whispered, awed at the thought.

"There are also shops that sell pretty things young women like," he said conspiratorially.

"Danarin, stop teasing," she laughed.

They finished lunch and set off again. Aldren started songs hunters often sang on the trail to pass the time and stave off boredom. He took care to avoid the raunchier lyrics sung only among men.

Here we stroll along the plains, tall and strong and true,

Our arrows fly as fast as wind and hit the target true!
South Peak sons are we, oh, South Peak sons are we!
We always do our fathers proud and love our women true!
South Peak sons are we, oh, South Peak sons are we!

When Aldren started a song about snakes in the tall grass, Naria threw a handful of berries at him.

"I forgot about the snakes, pretty one; I'm sorry."

He gave an exaggerated bow in apology that made Doonay frown at Aldren's 'pretty one' comment.

She snorted indelicately. "Pretty one? You must mean someone else who doesn't walk around in a stained, tattered tunic and hair that a bird would be happy to nest in."

Danarin sighed at the banter.

"Do we need to stop?" Tholan asked, solicitous of the older man.

Danarin shook his head and waved them on. Would it appear that three young men would now vie for her affection? Naria was unaware of her pretty face and sweet spirit, which added to her allure. There was no way to tell what would happen when they arrived in a town with thousands of young men.

***

That night, they camped on the open plains.

"I don't like this. There're no trees for cover, and fire is visible for a league or two," Doonay noted.

"It's like this the rest of the way. We can take turns watching the camp during the night," Danarin said.

Between themselves, Tholan and Aldren decided to make supper.

"I've seen my mother cook often enough," Aldren declared.

Not to be outdone in any matter, Doonay joined the discussion, and a friendly argument ensued over jerky, bread rounds, and "some odd root."

Naria was too tired to care, so she settled on her bedroll with a honey cake and trail mix. The last thing she heard before falling asleep was Aldren asking, "Does this look done?"

She seemed to have just fallen asleep when she felt a nudge on her shoulder. She blinked heavily and saw Doonay's grinning face above hers. All the men stopped what they were doing when she stretched, groaned, and greeted him with a husky morning voice.

Aldren decided mornings weren't so bad when greeted with that first thing in the morning. Maybe women on the trail could become an accepted practice.

On all that is sacred, does she have any idea how beautiful she is? Tholan thought.

What I wouldn't give to wake to that every morning for the rest of my life, Doonay mused.

"Planning to sleep through breakfast, sleepyhead?" he asked and gave her a bread round smeared with purple paste.

She sportingly took a bite and found it tasted awful. She coughed and took a long drink of water. "I've never had larin root that way," she said diplomatically. *At least they tried!*

"Larin root? What is its use? I don't think it goes with bread," Aldren asked.

"You're right. It has uses apart from food."

"Like a medicine?" Tholan asked.

"Yes," she replied shortly.

Larin root was in a brew for women to ease their monthly cycles' discomforting effects. As her mother would say, she didn't want to reveal that because it wasn't information for men's ears.

"What medicine?" Tholan asked.

Aren't you the curious one?

"This is an opportunity to learn from you," Danarin said.

She rolled her eyes and spoke. "It's used in a drink to help us ease the aches of our monthly cycles."

They dropped their paste-laden bread like it had burned their fingers and looked away.

"Well, you asked," she mumbled.

They packed camp and resumed their journey, and the day's sweltering heat made even the stalwart Doonay grumble. Naria donned her shawl to shelter her head and neck from the sun.

"Just last week, Mother mentioned she hadn't experienced this heat in years," Tholan said and shook his water skin to check the remaining amount.

"Those fools just had to take our horses, didn't they!" Aldren declared and poured water on the back of his neck.

"We can buy horses at Baranos. Good thinking, Aldren, it'll make our journey easier," Danarin said.

During the day, she had kept a sharp eye for wildfowl to snare but saw none. They still had a day's travel left; the remaining food was berries, trail mix, three bread rounds, and jerky.

***

That night, when they camped by a lake, she set snares in case any fowl approached the lake. She resumed cooking duty and made a proper jam from the berries and an herb sauce for the jerky. Although they were by a lake, she would fish in the morning because she was too tired. Would heat and hunger become a common occurrence in her life?

"Watch the snares; something might come for water. It's so barren here; I feel little energy from this country," she remarked.

"Except the heat," Doonay mumbled.

"The Wasted Plains is the name of this region," Danarin stated.

"Why is it named that?" Tholan asked.

Danarin explained, "According to ancient lore, the Great One over-looked this place during the creation of our world. The people who discovered it called it a waste of a god's time."

She took her flute from her pack, played a few notes, and lowered the flute. "While you bathed back at the village, I saw a fresh grave. It was old Brillon, the potter."

"I'm ashamed for not noticing it," Danarin said.

"Have no fear, father performed the last rites; I felt it," she assured him.

"He was very sick anyway, and when the invaders came, it was probably too much for him," Tholan added.

"I'll play a song to honor Brillon's spirit," she said.

The tune was comforting as it echoed across the barren, uncomfortable plain.

"Play another?" Doonay requested when she finished.

"I have another song in mind about the sons of South Peak."

"I've never heard it as music," Aldren commented.

She played the tune and continued to another when they settled on their bedrolls. After they fell asleep, she played well into the night.

***

She repeatedly cast her net the following morning and caught nothing but weeds. Feeling put out, she snatched the net from the water and stuffed it in her pack. The men wisely said nothing when they noticed her foul mood. The sun had barely been up for an hour, and she felt drenched. *Is there any shade in this cursed place?* Her foot was stinging, and she slipped off her slipper to find that her foot was red and swollen from insect bites. Danarin crouched, examined it, and felt her head.

"You're feverish too; that explains your sour mood," he sighed.

"I think the bites have made me sick. I have what I need to make a salve," she said.

"Make extra," Aldren added, and displayed red welts on his neck.

"Is anyone else bitten?" Danarin asked.

The rest shook their heads.

"The bugs found us tasty," Aldren quipped.

Her feverish body shuddered, and she felt nauseous but found focus on the thought of treating her first patient. She cupped the warm, brackish water of the lake in her hands and shook her head. *This water will not do.* She grasped her staff, closed her eyes, and prayed. *Spirits of the sky, we are in need. A good man of my people needs healing. I ask for rain and a cool breeze that may help ease his pain.*

They heard the rumble of thunder, a breeze blew into the camp, and cool rain fell. *Father was right; all you need to do is ask nicely.*

"We need to catch the water," Danarin instructed.

They made folds in the top flaps of their packs and placed their bowls and water skins below the folds. The rain collected in the folds and dripped steadily into the bowls. In minutes, five bowls were full of fresh water.

"How long will the rain last?" Danarin asked as they put their water skins in place of the bowls.

The glow in her eyes faded, and she eased the tight grasp on her staff. "As long as it's needed."

After she worked her mortar and pestle, her bowl was full of the medicinal salve, with more than enough for Aldren and her. After, she mixed soothing herbs in the extra bowls of water. She first applied the balm to Aldren's neck, then to her foot.

"I know of a way to make shade for these two until their fevers stop," Tholan offered. "We can stick our arrows into the ground and drape our bedrolls over the arrows."

The patients settled in the shade, and Naria placed the herb-soaked cloth on their foreheads.

"I must seem like a helpless infant," Aldren said.

She chuckled and asked, "How do you feel?"

"The pain in my neck isn't as bad as it was. The smell on this cloth makes me feel better too."

Travelers

S he woke up and was puzzled that Aldren wasn't lying beside her, then heard him talking to Danarin. Her foot still itched but was no longer swollen and painful, so she rolled from under the makeshift tent.

"While you were sleeping, a traveler stopped here. We talked and shared lunch, and he told us of a newer settlement called Eastwater not an hour away from here. It'll be nightfall by then. We'll be able to refill our water stores and rest," Danarin said.

"People live in this wretched land?" Aldren asked.

"Just watch what you say when we arrive," Danarin said.

When they arrived at Eastwater, they found the people were neither hostile nor friendly, but reserved. Someone showed them where they could refill their water skins and make camp. When an older man approached the companions, Danarin rose to greet him.

"We have food to sell if you're hungry," he stated.

"Thank you, but we carry what we need. Our people use no money, and we have nothing of value to barter," Danarin replied and sat again.

No one needed to know the fortune of gems they carried. The man nodded and turned, but not before seeing the marks on Naria's arm in the campfire light.

"You there, girl, are you a druid?" he demanded.

Doonay rose and spoke. "I would have you care about how you speak to this young woman."

That was as polite as he could be toward the coarse man, prompting the others to stand, to have his back if necessary.

"*Hmph*. Are you her father?" the man asked Danarin.

"I act in her father's stead," Danarin replied.

"Does she speak?" he asked.

Danarin nodded and gestured for her to approach.

She clasped her hands in front of her, as she had seen her father do numerous times, and spoke respectfully. "I am Druid, elder. What is it you ask of me?"

Her courtesy visibly took the man back, prompting him to speak more cordially. "I am the leader of a people who live a hard life in a hard land. We have little and are wary of strangers. That's the reason for my rough attitude."

Naria nodded her head for him to continue.

"Our worthless druid left for that blasted town weeks ago and never returned. This morning, the one who acts as a healer and three of our children became sick from insect bites. The healer himself is too sick to treat them. Do you have healing skills?"

She held her tongue at his "worthless Druid" comment, realizing that the emotions were probably running higher than usual if the village had sick ones.

"Yes, I have some healing skills. One of my companions and I were ill this morning from insect bites. It's fortunate that I still have enough healing salve for your people. I'll see to them."

***

The man led Danarin and her to a thatch-roofed wooden cabin. Inside, a man and three children were sweating and twitching uncomfortably on cots. She went to the man first.

"Children first," he gasped.

"Do you have a water basin and some cloth?" she asked the coarse man. He nodded to a woman standing at the tent entrance that hurried out.

Naria kneeled by the first child. "Hello handsome, what's your name?"

"Lerim," he replied weakly.

"I'm Naria, and I'm here to help you. Where did the bugs bite you?"

"My belly."

"What a troubling place for bites! I'm going to put some of this paste on your stomach to make the bites go away."

She raised his shirt and applied the salve to the bites, and his legs twitched.

"Are you ticklish?"

The boy nodded and smiled weakly.

"I'll try not to tickle you too much," she said conspiratorially.

"When will I get better?" he asked.

"When you're hungry and not feverish, you'll be all better," she replied.

She tickled his cheek, winked, and moved to the next boy. "My goodness, another handsome boy!" she said, and repeated the process.

The woman returned with a large water bowl, and Naria kneeled next to the girl. "What a pretty girl! What's your name?"

"Alenya."

"Like the flower, a pretty name for a pretty girl. How old are you?"

"Eight."

"Can you tell me where the nasty bugs bit you?"

"My legs."

"What a bothersome place, especially for children that like to play! Do you like to play?"

The girl nodded. The man and woman observing wrung their hands and watched intently.

"Good, I like to play too, so I'm going to put this paste on your legs to make the bites go away."

She finished with the children and kneeled next to the healer.

"You did good with the little ones; the fever is bad with them," he said.

"I hope to do good with you too," she said. "What's your name?"

"Taiel."

"Taiel, which means light in the old language. Where were you bitten?"

"S'not proper."

"Not proper? I don't understand," she said.

He gestured her closer and whispered in her ear. She blushed and resumed her kneeling position.

"That's unlucky," she said kindly and patted his shoulder. "I'll put the salve in your hand. Can you apply it?"

She rose and spoke to the others. "The bites are in a private area. He will apply the salve himself, but I must ask that we step out for his privacy."

"Of course," Danarin said.

After a minute, Taiel called out that he had finished. Naria prepared the water bowl with soothing herbs and soaked the cloths in the water, then placed a cloth on the forehead of each patient.

"It smells good," the little girl said.

"I want all of you to sleep. When you wake, you'll feel better."

She instructed the man and woman to keep the cloths wet with the soothing water on their heads until their fevers broke.

"One last thing," she said, taking her staff from Danarin.

She closed her eyes and bowed her head. They could see her eyes glowing under her closed eyelids, and the tent cooled inside. She opened her eyes and let out her breath.

"She is truly a druid!" the woman whispered.

"How long will it last?" the man asked in amazement.

"As long as it's needed," she replied.

When she returned to her companions, Danarin spoke proudly of her. "If only your father were here to see it. What you did was wasn't easy."

"It wasn't. I don't enjoy seeing children so sick and that poor man with bites in the worst possible place," she said.

***

That evening, four villagers approached the companions with a haunch of roasted deer on a spit, and a woman followed with a platter of steaming vegetables.

"We can't thank you enough for what you did. Fate sent you to us, so we offer this in gratitude."

There was no polite way to turn down the gracious offer of food, and she expected no payment for what she did. She knew her companions were already salivating at the sight of the savory food after days of trail mix. She rose, clasped her hands in front of her, and inclined her head.

"I accept this gracious offer. I'm happy to be of service to you."

After supper, Doonay patted his stomach and relaxed on his bedroll. Next to him, Naria combed her hair.

"I certainly hope you're full; you ate enough for five men. There's nothing left but bones," she said and nodded at Aldren and Tholan, dueling with rib bones.

"My belly is full because of you. You did something good and rewarded for it," he praised.

"I didn't do it for a reward. Those people were sick, and I did it freely."

"I know; the goodness in you pleases me," he said.

She took one of his large hands in her small ones. "Thank you for what you said today," she said and kissed the palm of his hand.

He sat up. "I'll have words with any man who doesn't treat you right."

"I've never had an older brother to take up for me before. Wait till I tell Father; he'll be so pleased," she teased.

"Older brother? I hope you see me as more than your brother, because I see you as more than a sister," he fussed.

"I know, I'm teasing."

She leaned forward and gave him a gentle, lingering kiss.

"I would never kiss a brother like that."

At sunrise, the companions ate a quick meal and shouldered their bags. A group of villagers approached them. The sick children, now good as new, stepped forward and gave her bunches of wildflowers. The healer stepped forward and extended his hands. She took them in return and felt something placed in her hand. It was a golden bracelet.

"Please accept it, young druid. If you ever pass this way again, know that you'll be welcome," he said.

The village leader stepped forward. "That's right; you'll be welcome. We know your people ran into trouble. We hope things are made right for you."

Danarin spoke. "Thank you for your kind words and hospitality. May the spirits be with you."

They left the village, and Danarin pointed in the distance. "If you look carefully, you'll see the roads to Baranos. We should arrive this afternoon."

***

The closer they got to Baranos, the more people they saw walking from all directions, on horseback, on horse-drawn carts, and guiding cattle pulling large wagons. When they set foot on the road, they came upon a gray stone tower as tall as a tree, with two guardsmen atop it.

"Good day to you!" she called.

"To you as well, pretty miss, welcome to Baranos!" a guard called back.

They passed five more towers before reaching the town's walls, also as tall as trees. Danarin led them to a shaded spot in a small grove near the town entrance.

"Wait here until I return. I need to inquire about the magistrate."

"What's a magistrate?" Aldren asked.

"He's like the chief elder of the town. He'll be able to help us best."

"Take care, elder," Doonay said.

While Danarin was gone, the myriad of people visiting the town amused the companions. A fancy horse-drawn carriage stopped at the entrance, and three scantily clad dancers gaily emerged from the carriage.

Aldren cleared his throat. "Now, there's something I've never seen before."

Naria scoffed. "Those women are barely dressed! It's indecent!"

"We'll probably see more of that," Aldren said solemnly, but amusement tinted his voice.

"Such an eyesore; we must be strong to withstand it," Tholan added, prompting the men to laugh.

There were no words for the next sight when a sizeable cattle-drawn wagon stopped at the entrance. A dozen dirty, forlorn men clad only in loincloths emerged from the wagon, joined at the waists by chains. A man prodded them through the gate entrance with a whip and shouted, "Move along, lazy sods!"

Stunned speechless, Naria averted her eyes. She had never seen such a pitiful sight or men with as little clothing on their bodies as the bunch.

"What the devil do you think that was about?" Aldren asked.

"I think that's punishment," Tholan said.

"They could at least punish them with their clothes on," Doonay added.

Another hour passed; Naria played her flute, Tholan carved on a piece of wood, and Doonay and Aldren talked about a past hunt.

"I think you must be mistaken; it was my arrow—"

"Danarin comes," Naria said and set aside her flute.

The elder waved as he approached with two sacks and sat down. He up-ended one, and a dozen elppa fruits dropped.

"It's been weeks since I've had a fresh elppa!" she exclaimed and chose one.

He took two loaves of bread, a hunk of cheese, and a dozen sweet, spongy cake rounds from the second sack and held up a more significant water skin.

"I saved the best for last... milk!" he declared.

They dove for the bowls in their packs. He observed the young people eat and tease each other, and felt a little less melancholic that they could still find joy in something as simple as milk. When the journey started, he thought they were too young to face such a difficult situation with such an uncertain outcome. They knew and accepted the situation, and left their homes and everything they knew with youthful optimism.

He remembered Nidale's parting words that fateful morning. "Remember, elder; everything happens for a reason. Fate isn't as fickle as you think."

In South Peak, he was one of the dozen elders who handled the village's affairs. He rarely had prolonged personal interaction with the younger population in his two years as an elder. That was best left to their parents, but now he was in the thick of youthful enthusiasm. He had seen the lazy, belligerent youth of the village, but fortunately, they weren't in this group. He now knew why the elders chose them.

At twenty-one, Tholan was already considered an artisan among the people. Because he was the only male among five sisters at home, he had a better insight into feminine sensibilities than the others, which would explain his affable demeanor with Naria. Quietly confident and well-spoken, he brought balance to the group.

Of the South Peak hunters, nineteen-year-old Doonay stood out as a leader, undoubtedly a future elder. Physically, he was the strongest of the group, and no one could doubt his courage. His mother had died giving birth to him, the youngest of four boys. His father had done his best to raise them, but he raised them without the gentling aspect of a mother's touch. One hoped that age and experience would cure him of speaking carelessly, so Doonay's most prominent problem (or learning experience, as Danarin viewed it) was Naria. Overwhelmed by her sensibilities, he had little idea how to respond.

Aldren, also nineteen and Doonay's best friend since childhood, brought a sense of light-heartedness that was welcome among the group. He would make an excellent entertainer if he weren't such an outstanding hunter. A keen observer of behavior, he was always ready with a song, amusing story, or droll anecdote. He distracted his family with practical jokes that were already legend among the people. Aldren would always be like the sun on a cloudy day.

His thoughts came to rest on Naria, the youngest of the group at eighteen. She was gaining a sense of wisdom beyond her eighteen years that was abruptly forced upon her. She should be back at her home enjoying the attentions of suitors, laughing with her mother over a cooking fire, and gossiping with her friends. She should be walking the plains and woods with her father, learning all she could about the Druid Path. It must have been frightening for her to return to the destroyed village, empty of those she loved. How helpless she must have felt, with all her power, that she couldn't do anything to help them. She had no choice but to trust her companions and wander about the realm with them.

They respected his opinion and trusted his judgment because he was an elder. In their eyes, he was the authority about everything in the world because he was an elder. He knew that wasn't true by a long shot, but if that brought a sense of comfort to his young charges, so be it. They needed all the reassurance he could offer in this uncertain time. Naria startled him when she waved her hand in front of his face.

"Elder, are you well?" she asked.

"Lost in my thoughts is all," he said.

"What happened in town with the masgerate?" Doonay asked.

"We meet with the magistrate tomorrow," he answered. "Today, we'll find lodging and explore the town. Remember my warning, but don't feel you must always look over your shoulder. Just stay alert."

BARANOS

They entered Baranos and paused in wonder at what they saw. It was a colorful town, bustling with more people than they had ever seen, milling about, doing many things. Shops lined the streets, selling everything a person could want or need. Wandering vendors hawked their wares, children chased stray dogs, and women opened windows to call for their loved ones. Armed, uniformed men patrolled the streets and looked at the plainsmen's simple leather tunics and trousers. They noticeably stood taller, even Naria, and more powerfully built than most townspeople. Danarin led them to a food vendor, a woman with a loud but friendly voice who shooed away a stray dog. She saw Danarin and gave him a large, flirty smile.

"So, you've returned! My, you're a bunch of large, brawny lads! Too bad I'm old enough to be your mother!" she exclaimed and fanned her face.

Tholan dropped his pack in shock at the comment. For once, he could think of nothing to say. What could he say to such a bold comment coming from an older woman? Doonay and Aldren bore blushing, bewildered looks on their faces. Naria pressed her face against Doonay's back to hide her growing laughter.

"Since Dan here—"

They looked at each other pointedly. *Dan??*

"—offered me a gem in trade for food; you can come back here and get as much as you want while you're here. It's the best in town!" she declared.

"Those powerful bodies of yours need a lot of nourishment," she added with a wink.

She gave Danarin a long, approving look from head to toe, which wasn't subtle. She made a brief kneading motion with her hands and soothed the fabric of her apron at her hips and stomach; she had never seen a man at his age in such fit condition! Naria had never come across someone as outrageous as the woman. Her effect on her companions was the funniest thing she had ever seen.

Danarin nudged Aldren, who quickly spoke. "Uh... thank you... miss?"

The others nodded and thanked her as well.

"Since you can afford the best, I suggest *The Setting Sun* for lodging. You go down that street to the first left until you come to a sign with a picture of the sun. Go in and tell them that Rillorna sent you," she instructed.

They turned to leave and paused when she asked, "Who's this that's been hiding behind you?"

"This is the Druid Naria, daughter of Nidale and Leeda," Danarin answered.

Naria pulled back her shawl, clasped her hands, and nodded. "Good afternoon, madam."

Rillorna put a hand over her heart. "My goodness, a flower among the weeds! How old are you, child?"

"Eighteen, madam."

"So polite! You were raised right," she said knowingly.

"I strive to be a dutiful daughter," Naria replied courteously, not knowing where the conversation was heading.

"Of course, you do, dear. You must return for afternoon tea," Rillorna suggested.

"If you wish it, I will," Naria replied.

"Wonderful! Now run along and rest from your travels," Rillorna said.

***

On the way to their lodging, they spoke of the horses they would like to buy, not yet reconciled to the distasteful practice of buying and selling the animals.

"Let Naria talk to them; she could probably charm the mangiest nag into a mare fit for a king," Aldren said and nudged her. "We were big, brawny lads until she showed her face, then we were weeds."

"That woman was outrageous," Naria said.

"You disapprove?" Aldren asked.

"Not at all. She's outspoken and made me laugh. She likes Danarin too."

"Likes him? The way she looked —" Tholan said.

"Really looked," from Doonay and Aldren.

"— at him was like he was something delicious she wanted to eat," Naria said, giggled.

"All right, that's enough elder teasing," Danarin said gruffly. "Look, here we are, The Setting Sun."

Inside the inn, the proprietor was dubious at the sight of the tall, quiet plainsmen. However, that all changed when the well-spoken elder introduced himself and produced a gem. He approached the companions and warmly greeted them.

"Please pardon my hesitation on your arrival. All kinds of people make their way into my establishment, but obviously, you are people of culture. I am Dallad Orvez, and I bid you welcome to *The Setting Sun*."

"Many thanks for your hospitality," Danarin said and placed a green gem in Dallad's hand. "We will take two men to a room and the young woman, her own."

The man clasped his hands together and bowed his head at Naria. "How lovely," he said and held his arm for her. "Permit me to show you the ground-level accommodations."

She nodded, took his arm, and politely listened as he gave the inn's history. She didn't know what *accommodation* meant, but the meaning would become apparent if she paid attention to the fancy man.

"... and this is the main dining area, or you may prefer to dine in our gardens," he said and led them to tables and chairs situated among flora and fauna.

"On the fifth and sixth nights of the week, we host entertainers for the enjoyment of our guests."

"Entertainers, you say?" Aldren asked.

"Oh yes, those gifted as bards, storytellers, and musicians," Dallad confirmed.

"I'd like to see that. After all, we are people of culture," Aldren said sagely, humor lighting his eyes.

"Splendid, the entertainment starts shortly after supper. Would you like to see your rooms?"

"Pardon me, Master Orvez, when is tea time?" she asked.

"There are two times, my dear. Morning tea is between breakfast and lunch, so can you guess the second time?"

She thought for a moment. "My guess is... the time between lunch and supper?"

"Precisely. Now to your rooms."

When she settled in her room, she sat in an oversized, comfortable chair and looked around. She had never been in such splendor. The bed looked luxurious, with a plump feather pillow, satin sheets, and plush blankets. She all but shocked the life out of herself when she saw her reflection in the full-size mirror. A curtain was hiding what appeared to be a large wash bin in the corner. She looked at herself in the mirror again. *Well, my tunic needs washing. How convenient to have a place to wash my things right here in the room!*

When someone knocked on the door, she looked through the peephole and saw Danarin on the other side. She opened the door for him to enter.

"Are you settled? Is everything to your liking?" he asked.

"It's very nice, but too much," she replied.

"Enjoy the comfort while you can. I see you've discovered the bath bin."

"Bath bin? I thought it was for clothes!"

As he laughed, two women arrived and curtsied quickly outside the door, each with a bucket of steaming water. A man nodded and entered with large, heated stones he set under the wash bin.

"We'll return, miss, with more water," one said.

"Do you still plan to take tea with Rillorna?" he asked.

"Yes, she was kind enough to offer, and she may be helpful while we're here," she said.

"The others want to explore the town a bit, so I'll go with you. Enjoy your bath."

She was almost asleep in the hot, scented water, but the sensation of a strange power seeping into the room roused her instead. She jumped from the bath and clutched her staff defensively against her chest. The feeling faded, and she realized she was shivering, nude, and dripping wet in the middle of the room. While settling a hairband after her bath, she became alarmed by banging on the door. She looked through the peephole and saw Doonay lift his hand to bang on the door again. She snatched open the door.

"Doonay, you don't have to beat on the door like you're trying to break it down!"

The men snickered at her fussing and Doonay's resulting embarrassment. She shouldered her satchel and took her staff in hand.

"I'm sorry," he said sheepishly.

"I don't mean to fuss, I was just surprised," she explained.

He extended his arm, much as Dallad had done earlier. "You smell good now."

She quickly sniffed the collar of her tunic. *Does that mean I usually smell bad?*

Danarin grimaced in exasperation at Doonay. Once downstairs, he told the men to be back in time for supper while he and Naria went to Rillorna's for tea.

***

Throughout the town, business slowed at teatime. The outside kiosk was closed at the woman's home, and her cottage door was open. Danarin rang a little hanging bell on the door frame.

"Come in!" a voice called from inside.

They stepped into a parlor where a pot of steaming tea, three cups, and a plate of small, round cakes were on a table.

"Welcome!" Rillorna called out when she came into the parlor.

"Thank you for your invitation. Tea is a tasty but rare luxury in our village," Danarin said.

"Let me take your cloaks. Why don't you have a seat and tell me about your village?"

Danarin told her about South Peak and his role as an Elder, and then Naria spoke of her family. "I'm the only child of Nidale and Leeda. My father is a druid, as were seven generations before him. My mother is one of the women's council leaders and the daughter of an elder before his death. I also have three uncles and an aunt."

"I've only seen one druid in my lifetime, here in town, but I'm not sure that he's even a real druid. You are one, so it's an honor to have you here," Rillorna said.

Naria didn't understand. "What do you mean by saying he's not even a real druid?"

"He may have been a druid at one time, but now he's nothing but a charlatan," Rillorna explained.

Naria knew what that word meant. Her father used it sometimes. "This man is pretending to be one? That's disgraceful." *The spirits must be angry with this pretender!*

"Many in this town pretend to be something they're not for greed and power," Rillorna said.

Danarin told her why they were in town, and Rillorna nodded her head in understanding.

"If there's any news to be had, the magistrate will hear of it. He'll be interested to know about a bunch of villains roaming the plains, preying on hapless people. Justice will come to you and your loved ones. Trust fate for that," she said, patting Naria's hand.

"Why don't you tell us of yourself?" Naria asked.

Rillorna waved her hand. "There's not much to tell. My two sons are in the town guard, and my husband and daughter passed away four years ago from fever sickness. I own this home and make a good living from cooking."

"I'm sorry for your loss. My wife and daughter passed on two years ago," Danarin said.

Naria remembered that day, the day after she turned sixteen. Danarin's twelve-year-old daughter, a bit of an explorer, wandered beyond the village's borders. She fell into a deep part of the river and drowned. Danarin's wife took her own life three days later, unable to bear the grief.

"But here you are, in the stead of this girl's father and those young men, being a father again. It's a good thing you're doing, Danarin," Rillorna said.

"It's easy with this one, but the young men are another matter," Danarin added.

"Do any of them catch your pretty eyes?" Rillorna asked.

Naria blushed and took a bite of her sweet cake.

"Ah, woman talk," Danarin said and stood up.

"You don't mind, do you?" Rillorna asked.

"Not at all; the poor girl has been alone with men most of the week," he said.

"She'll be safe with me, and we might do a bit of shopping. What do you say? Do you like pretty things?"

Naria smiled and nodded eagerly. "Yes, I do!"

"Then I'll return later to take her back for supper," Danarin said.

When he left, Rillorna refilled her cup. "You seem uneasy. Is it hard to talk about your young man?"

Naria cleared her throat and spoke. "I don't have a young man yet. Sometimes I think my companions compete because of me. I don't want to cause them not getting along; this is the worst possible time for it."

"Men will be men, no matter the time or place," Rillorna advised sagely.

"My mother says that. Of the three with me, I've been friends with one of them since we could walk. We've shared some kisses, and he's interested in more, but...."

She paused, played with the frayed ends of her shawl, and let out a shuddering breath.

"Take your time, dear," Rillorna advised.

"He says things that hurt my feelings, but he doesn't know it hurts. I try to be patient, but it's hard to be patient all the time. I hate I get angry with him...."

She stopped and let her hands fall to her lap. "Sometimes, I feel he expects me to be with him no matter what he says or does. That's not fair to me, is it? Am I whining?"

"No, you're a young woman exploring your heart," Rillorna said.

"I care for him and don't want to hurt him. I think he's trying to make me believe that he's the only man in the world for me," Naria said.

"Then tell him all you've told me," Rillorna said.

"He won't understand."

"If he doesn't, he'll have to learn to live without you until he understands."

"It can't be that simple," Naria returned.

"Of course it can; it's called tough love," Rillorna said, patting her hand. "Now, finish up your tea. A bit of shopping should cheer you right up."

"Tough love?"

"Yes. Doing what's good for someone you care for, even though you know how hard it'll be."

The Beer

Before they left the cottage, Naria took her pouch of gems from her knapsack and dumped them on the table. In her heart, she knew she could trust Rillorna.

"Please explain to me the value of these gems; I don't understand it."

Rillorna fanned her face, looked out a window as if she expected someone to be peering in, and urged Naria to put the gems back into the pouch quickly. "First, you mustn't take all those out like that! There are those in this town who would rob you blind! But for the sake of knowledge, the blue ones are called sky gems. They're worth the most, more money than I can think of, and I can think of a lot! Only royals and nobles have those."

She held up a green one. "These are worth less than the blue ones, but still very valuable. They're called earth gems."

She shook her head in amazement at the sight of all the gems. "The red ones, called fire gems, are worth the least, but still an impressive amount. Danarin gave me a red gem for food, and I feel like I'm taking advantage, but he assures me I'm not. Thanks to that little red gem, I can retire if I like."

"He gave the inn owner a green one. You're not taking advantage; Danarin wouldn't let that happen. Each of us has dozens of them," Naria said.

"Dallad probably thinks you're some nobility just to whip out a gem," Rillorna chuckled.

"What about these clear ones?"

"Just glass, good only for decoration. Now, let's get you some pretty things."

"Can I exchange a gem for money?"

"Do you have a cart? Because you'll need it to carry the coin you'll get for it! You can start an account at a bank if you deposit the gem, and get coin based on the worth of the gem," Rillorna said.

"All these coin matters seem so complicated," Naria complained.

"But necessary because you can't keep all that money on your person or at home. It's not safe."

***

Later, they left the bank, Naria with a pouch of gold coins on her belt, with another two in her knapsack. One of the young bankers asked her to supper, and the chief banker promised prompt interest earnings on her account, whatever that meant. Naria bought a new bedroll, pillow, and a small tent throughout the morning. To her surprise, she came across a shop that sold herbs and such to replenish her supply.

"Aren't you concerned about the weight you'll be carrying?" Rillorna asked.

"It's not heavy to me, and we're buying horses. They'll lighten the load," Naria answered.

She paused and closed her eyes when she felt another surge of energy, similar to the one that interrupted her bath. She felt Rillorna gently shaking her shoulder.

"Are you all right?" the older woman asked.

"I felt power different from my own," Naria replied.

"Does it hurt?"

Naria pinched the bridge of her nose and massaged her temples. "No, but it's hard to describe how it feels."

"There's a wizard in the temple area."

Naria's eyes popped open. A wizard!

***

Danarin returned to Rillorna's and saw Naria's knapsack alongside a new bedroll, pillow, and tent. *Smart girl.* He heard townspeople talking excitedly and saw them running toward the direction of the temple. He heard a man exclaim "Magic fight at the temple!" and looked again at her belongings. Her staff wasn't there, which meant that she had it with her, a realization that prompted him to run toward the Temple Commons. He heard jeering and shouting, then Naria's loud, angry voice upon arrival.

"You vile man!"

He pushed through the crowd and saw Naria confronting an older man with marks on his arm like hers. Standing next to a priest, Rillorna was anxiously wrung a handkerchief. A wizard on his left stared at Naria, awestruck.

"Now see here, you impudent young—" the man spoke.

Naria raised her chin, not at all intimidated, and her eyes glowed with righteous anger. The older man took a step back and she shouted again. "You have no authority over me, worthless fraud! The spirits took back their gifts when you chose greed over your people! Where is your staff, pretender?"

He stepped away and raised his hands, further prompting Naria's anger.

"Yes, false one, let's see your skills! Let these people witness your lies. You've done worse than steal their money; you've stolen their hope! May the spirits have mercy on your foul soul!"

The man chanted while Naria glared at him in disgust, her eyes still glowing. He dropped his hands and looked nervously at the crowd. She closed her eyes, clutched her staff, and chanted words known only to her.

Thunder rumbled overhead, winds blew through the temple grounds, and heavy rain fell. When the pretender fell to his knees, Naria stepped back.

"Don't fear me, liar. Fear the spirits and beg for their mercy. Heed this warning," she warned.

The crowd dispersed while some lingered, hoping to speak to her, and the pretender ran from the temple area. She nodded to the priest and wizard and turned around. Danarin and Rillorna were amazed at the actions of the usually unassuming, soft-spoken young woman.

***

The companions sat at the best table in the gardens at supper time. A woman came to their table with a tray of decorative goblets and welcomed them to supper.

"Tonight, you can choose from fowl, beef, or lamb. Vegetables and bread come with the meal, and after, you choose sweet fig cake or creamed berries."

While waiting for the food, Danarin spoke of what happened on the temple grounds that day.

"I can't believe I missed that. Naria raised her voice, in anger, no less," Aldren teased.

"You must think I'm suddenly wrong in the head," she said to Danarin.

"I know you're not wrong in the head, but you saw an injustice and reacted. He's been taking advantage of people; that's bad enough, but even more so to you."

Tholan spoke up. "Naria, I found something for you today,"

He placed an object wrapped in a pink cloth in front of her. She unfolded the fabric and found a beautiful flute, larger and more ornate than her own.

"Thank you for both," she said, admired the fine wood of the flute and the smooth piece of shimmering fabric.

Danarin placed a piece of fabric in front of her with a smile. She pulled back the cloth to reveal an oval piece of wood engraved with an image of the plains, complete with mountains in the background.

"This is beautiful, thank you, elder," she said.

"I have something for you too," Aldren said, and gave her a decorated hairband.

"It's pretty as well, thank you," she said.

Doonay couldn't have felt any stupider. He and others bought themselves new boots, but they still thought of buying something for her. He hadn't, but she expressed no hurt or accusation, and she even admired his new boots.

Their food arrived, and they marveled over the richness of the meat and vegetables. After dessert, the musicians arrived, and prominent townspeople came to the inn to hear the music. They enjoyed the lively music, and servers brought trays of refreshments. She felt trapped in the crowded room and chose a seat by the window to see the night sky. A server brought a tray of drinks, and she chose one she'd never heard of: beer. Its pungent smell tickled her nose and had an interesting nutty, sweet taste. She took a long drink and patted her feet in time with the music. She felt rather good when she finished the glass, so she asked the server for another cup.

Danarin realized Naria was no longer sitting beside him halfway through the first song. He saw her by the large window, her eyes glazed over with a sleepy look. Her head would occasionally bob, causing her to giggle. She was humming and lazily waving her hand in time with the music.

"Something's wrong with her," Tholan said.

When they went to her table, she gazed at them with sleepy eyes, giggled, and spoke, "Look, it's the big brawny lads of South Peak," she slurred and winked.

"What the devil is wrong with her?" Aldren asked, astonished at the behavior of the best-behaved person he knew.

Danarin picked up her glass and sniffed it. "She doesn't know what beer is."

"Do you mean to say that she's drunk?" Doonay asked.

"Yes, Doonay, that's what I'm saying. I'll put her to bed; she needs to sleep. Time is the only remedy for this," Danarin said.

He helped her stand and made to guide her upstairs. She swayed, fell against him, and retched on his chest.

"And I thought to carry her," Aldren commented.

Tholan opened the door, entered the room, and pulled the bedcovers back. Danarin laid her on the bed and pulled the covers back over her. She mumbled something unintelligible and cuddled with the pillow.

***

When she woke, all she knew was that the sunlight streaming through the curtains was torture. Her mouth was painfully dry, and she had the most miserable headache of her life. She heard a soft knock on the door and trudged across the room to open it. She missed the door latch on the first try, and when she opened it on the second try, the room maids were there with buckets of hot water.

"For the bath, miss," one said.

She stepped aside to let them work. Danarin appeared at the door with a glass of water.

"It's just water, I promise."

She gratefully took the glass and drank.

"After a bath, you'll feel better, and I'll take you to Rillorna's for breakfast. This morning we buy horses. Aldren is excited."

"I have... had a pony," she said.

"Would you like to join us?"

"Maybe after I've finished my shopping. Rillorna and I enjoy each other's company."

He nodded in understanding, and the maids returned with more water.

"Enjoy your bath," he said and left.

During her bath, she remembered everything from the previous night. Her behavior mortified her. *Good heavens, what the men must think! I retched on Danarin! I've been in town too long. I need to feel the soil and grass beneath my feet, breathe in the plains' open air, and feel fresh water on my face!*

She left the inn with Danarin, avoiding the curious eyes of her companions. At Rillorna's, the older woman saw the unsettled, off-color look on Naria's face.

"Are you sick?" she asked.

"Not exactly. She discovered beer last night by accident," Danarin said.

"Vile drink. How was I to know?" Naria fussed.

Rillorna patted her shoulder. "It's a good thing I made porridge this morning; it's just the thing to settle your stomach."

"I'll return after lunch for our audience with the magistrate. No beer for you, young woman," Danarin playfully scolded and left.

Before leaving, Naria ate two bowls of porridge and helped clean the breakfast dishes.

"Rillorna, may we go outside the town for a while after shopping?"

"Feeling a bit hemmed in?"

"A bit, yes."

"We can have a nice picnic; how does that sound?"

"Good, thank you."

"What would you like to buy today?"

"Hmm... I'd like to get something for my companions and visit a tanner."

They walked along the street, perusing the various shops. Naria nibbled on a honeycomb from a wandering vendor and stopped at a shop that sold things men would like. She saw the selection of knives that would make perfect gifts for her companions. When she left the shop with the new blades, she asked Rillorna what a mercenary was.

"Why in the world do you ask that?" Rillorna queried.

"The shop owner asked if I was making good money as a mercenary," Naria replied.

"Someone hires a mercenary to kill people for money."

Naria felt appalled. "How dare he ask such a thing! I'm going to go back in there and give him a piece of my mind! I revere life!"

"Naria, he probably said it in jest. Don't fret over it."

"Perhaps he should find something else to jest about!"

The next stop was a cobbler. One look at her tattered rabbit-hide slippers (where her little toe was protruding from the left slipper) prompted her to go inside. She emerged from the shop with new, sturdy sandals on her feet. The thicker, sturdier soles and covered toes would make her travels easier on her feet, and they wouldn't slip off like the slippers. The tanner was situated away from the other shops at the street's end because of the smell. A woman scraping a bearskin stretched out on a table nodded at the two that entered the shop and continued her work. Naria browsed the shop's selection while Rillorna chatted with the tanner. She came to pieces of leather folded and stacked on a table and ran her hand over them. She had never felt such supple leather. *This would make a fine tunic!*

"See something you like?" Rillorna asked.

"This is the finest leather I've ever seen!" Naria remarked.

"Thank you, miss," the woman from the table said.

"What will you use them for?" Rillorna asked.

"Tunics and breeches," Naria said.

"No cloth? No pretty fabrics and colors?" Rillorna asked and looked at Naria's sleeveless leather tunic. She didn't know what to make of the knee-length breeches underneath, as she had never seen a woman wearing breeches.

"Don't worry. I'll use pretty fabrics for bedclothes and shawls. The tunic I'm wearing is a coming-of-age gift from my mother. With a long skirt and pockets, this style is a traditional symbol that I'm ready to assume the role of a homemaker. As a druid, well, it's what a druid wears."

"I understand. Leather is more durable than cloth, especially because you live on the plains," Rillorna said.

"Exactly," Naria replied.

"Might this be of interest?" the tanner asked and draped a thicker piece of leather over her arm. It was just as smooth as the leather she was holding, worked to a shine, and was a darker shade of brown.

"I'll take that for a new cloak," Naria said.

They finished shopping and returned to Rillorna's home to pack a basket for a picnic. When they settled in a shaded grove outside the town next to a creek, Naria closed her eyes and enjoyed the sound of water moving over the stones in the creek bed. A squirrel ran down a tree and greeted her with a busy chirping.

"Why in the world would a squirrel do that, I wonder?" Rillorna asked.

"He's my familiar," Naria said with a sigh, but she was glad to see the squirrel and gave it a bit of nut bread.

"I had hoped for something more impressive, like my father's hawk. There's a reason for everything, as he says. I just haven't figured out the reason for a squirrel. Aldren thinks I should name him Rat."

The squirrel chirped and flicked his tail in indignation, which prompted Naria to pat his head in comfort. "Don't worry, little friend. I'll think of a good name for you."

The Spoon

After the picnic, they returned to Rillorna's home and found Danarin waiting.

"I'm glad to see you're feeling better," he said.

"Pleasant shopping and a picnic away from the town did a world of good," Naria said.

"We bought fine horses this morning. After we meet with the the magistrate, I'll take you to see them."

At the town hall, the companions waited to meet with the magistrate. Unless one of them asked a direct question, Danarin would do all the talking. A man wearing a gray satin tunic adorned with a pair of crossed swords ushered them into the magistrate's court. Guards, scribes, and other officials quieted when they approached, and the magistrate spoke.

"I understand that there's been some trouble with your village. Speak, plainsman."

Danarin nodded and told them of the events of the past week. The magistrate looked at his captain, who spoke. "I've heard or seen nothing of this alleged army. We have regular patrols that perform a day's long sweep of this region in all directions, and they've reported nothing of this rabble. If these ruffians took it upon themselves to make away with an entire village, I daresay they don't want anyone to know of it."

The magistrate spoke. "I agree. Hundreds of men, women, and children would be impossible to miss. This is truly troubling. What is to stop them from raiding other villages? Who is to say they don't have spies in this town as we speak? What do you suggest, captain?"

"That we send messengers with all due haste to the surrounding towns and villages. If we only had a description of these —"

He stopped talking when Naria's chin dropped to her chest, and she slumped against Doonay. He took hold of her to keep her from falling while Aldren caught her staff.

"Is the druid well?" the magistrate asked.

"Please give her a moment. She's a young druid and goes into trances unexpectedly," Danarin explained.

The magistrate directed a man nearby to bring her a cup of water and another to bring a chair. She came into awareness again and looked at Doonay, then Danarin with wide eyes.

"I saw them! The men who took our families!"

She had been praying for a vision, a sign, or anything that would be of help. The captain walked forward and snapped his fingers for a scribe to come forward.

"Tell us, young woman."

"They are men of all kinds," she said.

"What do you mean?" the captain asked.

"Except for me and my father, all our people have only dark hair and dark eyes. None of our men have hair on their faces or wear jewels. These men in my vision have all colors of hair and eyes, many have hair on their faces, and most of them wear jewels."

She thanked the cupbearer and took a sip of water before speaking again. "They wear green shirts, brown trousers, and brown boots. Some of them wear metal shields on their chests, while others wear the shields on their arms. There are strips of black cloth around their arms, adorned with embroidered or painted flames."

"Did you see our people?" Danarin asked gently.

She shook her head, and a tear rolled down her cheek. The captain cleared his throat and gave her a handkerchief.

"I saw our horses among theirs! They were frightened! Our horses are not horses for battle."

She looked at her companions. "They were burning figures onto their flanks!" she cried, horrified.

Doonay shook his head and patted her back in comfort.

"Devils," Tholan growled.

The captain told Danarin, "If we find a horse from your village, we need to know how they're marked."

"With dye that can't be washed off. A yellow circle on the right flank," Danarin answered.

"Is that all, young druid?" the magistrate asked.

"Yes sir," she replied sadly.

The magistrate addressed the captain. "Captain, send scouts about the territory with all due haste. Double the patrols, relay this story and the description of these ruffians. The prince needs to know of this as well. I'm sure he'll be interested to know that this has occurred in his realm."

He again addressed Danarin. "What are your plans?"

"We're going to the capitol; villages along the way might have seen or heard something of our people or the renegades. Once we get there, I'll try to speak with the prince."

"Excellent plan. I ask that you deliver my monthly dispatch to the capital since you're going there, anyway. That frees more men to patrol this region, and we're short of men as it is," the magistrate said. "Are you in need of anything for the journey? Supplies? Weapons? Horses?"

"We thank you, sir, but we have what we need," Danarin said.

"Very well. I wish you a better fortune for the future and a swift reunion with your families. Would you mind a bit of friendly advice?" he asked.

"I think we rather need it," Danarin replied.

"With my seal on the dispatch, you'll be granted an audience with the prince, so don't squander it. It's uncommon for commoners, especially strangers who stroll in from the plains. Tell him all you've told me and accept his help if he offers. I know that you're proud, independent people, but in this case, you need help to get your families back."

"We'll remember that. Thank you for your time and help," Danarin said, and the companions left the hall, wending to the ranches outside of the town beyond the eastern wall.

***

"Our horses are in the stables to the left," Danarin said.

Naria's spirit was lifted at the sight of the beautiful animals, and the seller welcomed them back.

"How did things go with the magistrate?"

"Better than expected," Danarin replied.

"Good to hear," the man said and gestured toward the horses. "They've been fed, watered, and brushed. The filly's been frisky, but you probably like your females frisky, heh?"

Doonay frowned at the man, who saw Naria and apologized. "Sorry, miss, didn't see you back there behind the saddles."

A filly came to the fence, pawed the ground, and flicked her tail. She was striking, solid black except for a white splash on her chest.

"Didn't you say the filly is for the miss?" the seller asked.

"She's mine? Can I walk her?" Naria asked, thrilled.

"She's yours; you can if you wish," Danarin said.

The seller gave her a rope, and she looped it around the filly's neck. A stable boy opened the gate, and she went into the pen, leaving the men to talk. She led the filly to the pasture beyond the pens, where she put her nose in the air and shook out her mane.

"It's better out here, isn't it? When the night sky—" she said and paused her rambling. "That will be your name, Night. You look like the night, solid black with a big star on your chest," she said and scratched the filly's neck.

Night whinnied softly and nuzzled her neck.

"We're going to be good friends. I get a female companion for the journey! I promise I won't be too much of a burden for you."

If horses rolled their eyes, Night did, as if to say *you, too much for this horse? Nonsense!* From a distance, the men watched Naria get to know the horse.

"She comes from good stock, that one," the seller said.

***

At supper, Naria gave the men the gifts of knives.

"A splendid gift, thank you," Danarin said.

"You should have been there when I told the shopkeeper I was interested in buying so many knives. He asked if I was a mercenary."

"I got you a gift," Doonay said and placed a decorative wooden cooking spoon in front of her. "Nice, isn't it?"

She had a brief mental image of hitting his head with it. *If I bring my arm down hard enough...*

"Yes, it's a good spoon. It's... useful, thank you," she replied politely.

Doonay looked pleased with himself, and Danarin decided to have a long talk with Doonay. Was he so unaware? He could tell that Naria was losing her patience with him.

If my father gave my mother a spoon as a gift, she'd break it over his head, Aldren thought.

My chances grow better with every word he speaks, with every move he makes, Tholan mused.

After supper, she excused herself for the night. She had some hard thinking to do. At her room, the maids drew a bath and lit the torches on the balcony. Lost in thought, she sat in the water until it cooled, her skin pruned.

I need to focus. I've lost some of it in this place, except I received a vision just when I needed it.

Thoughts of Doonay crept into her mind. *Maybe he's not the man of my heart... a spoon!?*

She huffed in frustration at her confusion, left the bath, and dressed for bed. She wrapped a blanket around herself and sat on the balcony. With a sigh, she looked at the clear night sky full of bright, blinking stars.

We leave for a four-day trek across the realm, to talk to a prince about the fate of a people he's never met, because of an unknown army. Do I need to be worrying about Doonay and a spoon?

She was startled from her musings by the appearance of her squirrel. She looked over the balcony to see how he got there and saw ivy running up the inn's wall. He performed his usual chirping and tail-flick greeting, sniffed her hand, and scurried into the room. He inspected each object in the room before scurrying up on the bed.

"Are you telling me I should be in bed? Should I call you Bedbug?"

The squirrel rose on his hind legs and chirped furiously, causing her to laugh. She laughed because talking to a squirrel was funny and having said squirrel fuss was just the fun she needed.

"I know what I'll call you! Your name will be Garil, which means moody in the old language," she said and sat on the bed.

The squirrel quieted and seemed to contemplate her for a moment.

"I have an uncle named Garil. I'd give anything to see him right now."

The squirrel climbed on her lap.

"You'll do for now."

***

The following day, the companions thanked the inn owner for an enjoyable stay and went to Rillorna's for a hearty breakfast. They had a long trip to start.

"Is there anything you can tell us about the journey?" Danarin asked Rillorna.

"No, I've never been more than a day's distance from this town. I'm a tad worried about this one, though; four days in the wilderness seems like a hardship," she said, patting Naria's hand.

"Please don't worry, I'm not. I would've made the trip, anyway. Druids travel to learn about the world and the people in it. I'm used to the wilderness; I'm comfortable there. Do you think these four will let anything happen to me?"

"Well, nothing better happen to you. Promise me you'll do your best to stay safe and come back to see me."

"We promise," Danarin affirmed.

Rillorna didn't mean to get so attached to them in such a short time, but she couldn't help it. Danarin was kind and wise, and the young men were so polite and forthright. They were covetous and protective of Naria, for good reason. She hoped with all her heart that things turned out well for them. When it was time to leave, Danarin instructed them to bring the horses to the town's entrance.

"I'll be along shortly," he said gruffly.

Rillorna bid them a warm goodbye, and when Naria received a lingering hug, she secretly slid a red gem into the woman's apron pocket before she stepped away. While saddling the horses, they speculated about Danarin's gruff instructions. The stable boy opened the gate, and the companions led the horses out to let them get used to the feel of the saddles.

"Not too heavy, is it?" Naria teased Night.

They walked the horses to the town entrance and waited. She fed Night an elppa, and Garil appeared, scampering down from a tree.

"Hey, it's Rat!" Aldren joked.

"Not Rat; it's Garil," Naria corrected and extended her arm to him.

He scampered up her arm and settled on her shoulder.

"A squirrel on a horse? What a bunch we are," Aldren commented.

"Isn't that your uncle's name?" Doonay asked.

"Danarin approaches," she said.

"I still think Rat is a better name," Aldren said.

"Let's head west," Danarin said with a sigh and took to his horse. "What about a rat?"

"Are you well, elder?" she asked when they settled in their saddles.

"In time, I will be," he said evenly and turned his reigns west.

THE CARAVAN

During the morning of their continued journey, no conversation was held. The companions were content to listen to the sound of their horse's hooves on the ground. They occasionally looked back until Baranos was no longer in sight. They stopped for lunch when the sun was at its highest point in the sky, and Naria removed an elppa and a book from her satchel.

"What's that?" Doonay asked.

"A book, obviously," she replied, sensing another thoughtless commentary from the hunter.

"But you can't read; none of our people read," he countered.

"Which is why I have this," she said, holding up the book. "Rillorna gave it to me. It's a book children use when they learn to read and write."

"Why would you want to do that?" he asked.

Here we go again, Danarin thought.

"To learn something new? Is that so bad?" she asked.

Doonay opened his mouth to reply, but was interrupted. "I see you bought a sword. Why would you do that? Do you plan to stab and slash at someone?" she retorted.

"Naria, simmer down. I'm sure Doonay meant no offense," Danarin advised.

"For someone who doesn't mean offense, he's doing a lot of it!" Naria snapped and regretted the comment a second later. "Elder, I'm sorry; that outburst was not aimed at you."

Aldren and Tholan looked at each other pointedly. Once again, Doonay stuck his large foot into his even larger mouth.

"I see this journey as necessary to rescue our families, but I see that it's also a learning experience with every hour that passes. Every druid strives to learn a new craft or skill to pass to the next one, and I've decided that reading and writing will be the skill I pass down."

She returned her attention to her book and threw a pointed glance at Doonay, daring him to say another word about it. Lunch continued in silence until Danarin announced it was time to continue.

***

As the sun set, they made camp beside a pond. There were no trees as far as they could see, but the land wasn't like the Wasted Plains. It was alive and flourishing with plenty of game, breezes, and clean, cold ponds. She hung a pot over a fire and started a stew. While it simmered, she assembled her tent, which prompted the others to look at each other and then her in surprise.

Why didn't I think of that? Tholan wondered.

"All I bought were these boots! They're fine boots, but won't keep the rain from falling on my face as I sleep!" Aldren declared, and Doonay wisely kept his mouth shut.

When her tent was set to her liking, she checked on Night and returned to the stew. She was satisfied with the progress and started on the honey cakes. She always enjoyed cooking, but now it seemed especially enjoyable when she needed something to occupy her thoughts. Her companions thanked her for supper and talked of their time in Baranos. She excused herself from the discussion, retrieved her staff, and assumed a meditative position away from the others facing north. Garil crouched next to her, perfectly still, and she closed her eyes to implore the heavens for peace of spirit. She cast her fears and frustrations to the wind, intoned a prayer for her parents, and asked for a blessing for Rillorna.

Danarin urged the three men to sleep while he watched over his meditating young charge, who had been praying and meditating for hours. *She must be distraught; I've never seen her meditate so deeply.* Occasionally, her shoulders would shake, and he heard a choked sob that made him stand up to go to her. She finally opened her eyes, took a deep breath, and let a handful of dirt fall from her hand. When she rose to go to her tent, he noted the trails of tears on her tired face. She took a cloth from her pack and started toward the pond to wash the day's grime from her face.

"Naria, are you well?"

She stopped and gave him a sad smile. Her answer echoed his earlier words. "In time, I will be."

***

The second day passed much like the first, except for more talk to pass the time. After lunch, Naria smiled at the memory of her new friend Rillorna.

"What makes you smile?" Aldren asked.

She chuckled and scratched Night's neck. "When Rillorna hugged me, I slid a gem into her apron pocket. I wish I could have seen the look on her face when she found it."

"I know of something to pass the time. We aren't skilled in the old language, but you are, Naria. Can you teach us while we journey?" Tholan asked.

She laughed again. "That will take more than a few days!"

"Just a few words?" Aldren asked.

"All right, I can teach you some basic words. Here's the first one, for a horse," she said and reached over to pat Night's neck. "Os'ghi."

She laid her hand on her chest. "Wev'a, woman."

They repeated after her, and then she pointed to Doonay. "Mev'a, man."

Again, they repeated the word.

"Mev'a fi wev'a yot os'ghi," she said.

"Have you been drinking beer again? Because that's what it sounds like," Aldren teased.

She rolled her eyes. "An extra honey cake goes to the one who can tell me what I just said."

"I've got it! Woman and man on horse?" Tholan offered.

"Tholan gets the prize," she said.

***

The third day's journey would be more eventful than the previous two. At midday, they spotted a stream running through a thicket in the distance where they would stop to eat and rest. When they arrived, a caravan of six large, cattle-driven wagons were settled between the thicket and stream. People and dogs milled about, not noticing the companion's approach. Danarin lifted his arm and called out a greeting. The people in the caravan stopped what they were doing and peered curiously at the five approaching on horseback.

"I'm Danarin, an elder of South Peak village, and these are my companions," Danarin said and gestured at the four. "May we share some of this ground for food and rest?"

The strangers looked at a man who thought for a moment and offered a quick nod. They took care of the horses and settled down for lunch, and Naria quizzed them with old language as they ate. Naria laughed when Doonay used the word for bread instead of dirt.

"Listen, my dultur," she deadpanned, "dirt is elif. Bread is sulin'ik, the meat is ollen'ik," she said.

"So ik on the end of a word means to eat?" Tholan asked.

"At least one of you is listening," she remarked and gave him another honey cake.

"What's dultur?" Doonay asked.

"Judging by her tone, I don't think it was a friendly word," Aldren noted.

They paused in their conversation when a dog from the caravan shyly approached the companions, licking his lips at the sight Tholan's jerky.

"Oh, all right, take it," he said and tossed it to the dog.

A young boy wandered close to the group and regarded them curiously. A woman from the caravan called out in alarm when she saw the child and ran to him.

"I apologize. His curiosity gets the best of him, and our meal was lacking," she admitted.

"Would you like to eat with us? We have more than enough to share," Danarin offered.

Naria nodded and smiled as she enjoyed meeting new people. The woman hesitated and relented when she saw her son gazing at their food.

"Very well, I'll let my husband know," she said, and minutes later, she returned with the boy. "He insists on paying you for your hospitality."

"No need for that; we freely share what we have," Danarin said.

"You're very kind, thank you," she said as she and the boy sat. "I am Zora Pillath, and this is my son, Kipton. We're from the port city of Hamaros, north of the mountains."

"We're pleased to meet you. I'm Danarin, an elder of our people. My companions are the hunters, Doonay and Aldren; the woodworker, Tholan; and the druid, Naria."

The boy was fascinated with the squirrel. "Is that your pet?"

He had never seen a pet squirrel; dogs, cats, and birds, but never squirrels as pets.

"I wouldn't call him a pet; he doesn't belong to me. He chooses to stay with me," Naria explained. "He's my familiar, named Garil. He probably sees me as his pet."

The boy laughed and pointed at her. "You're funny!"

The guests were served first. The boy tore into the bread, fruit, and cheese, appalling his mother.

"Kipton, mind your manners!" she scolded. The boy mumbled an apology through a mouthful of food.

"Manners aren't a matter to a hungry boy on the trail," Aldren said, winking at the boy.

"You mentioned that you're an elder of your people. What people?" Zora asked.

"The South Peak people," Tholan said. "We numbered over three hundred at one time."

"We still do," Aldren insisted. "We will find them, and we will restore our village."

Zora nodded. "I see... we know of your village, we've known it as *that village just beyond the mountains.*"

Danarin told Zora the tale that led them to where they were. Zora sighed and spoke. "And I thought we had the devil's luck. We left just over a week ago from Port Hamaros, on our way to Rylanos, as you are. I grant that it's not the tragic circumstances of your people, but we aren't faring well ourselves."

Zora smiled when Naria offered the boy a honey cake, and he scooted closer to the young woman.

"We're ambitious businesspeople, so we left in search of better fortune. After we passed through the mountains, our fortune soured. Four of our horses have died of a mysterious sickness, and our oxen have been ill at ease. As you can see, our wagons are damaged to where we cannot continue, but that's not the worst part," she said and covered her mouth.

"Yesterday, four of our group fell gravely ill and died during the night."

Naria gasped, hugged the boy, and felt his forehead.

"This morning, three more were found ill, and we fear the same fate for them. Our food stores are running dangerously low as well."

Naria looked at the sky and put a hand over her heart with a quick prayer. "Once again, Fate leads us where we need to be. Please permit me to be of service to your people. I have healing skills and offer last rites for those who have passed on."

"Our woodworker is skilled; he can be of use for your wagons," Danarin offered and Tholan nodded in agreement.

"What about us?" Doonay said, pointing to Aldren and himself. "We're among the best hunters of our people. There is much game here, and when we're done, your food stores will be full again."

"I'm overwhelmed by your offer. Please allow me to speak with our leader," she said.

"Here, take these back for the other children," she said and gave Zora a stack of honey cakes.

Zora went to the caravan and returned to the companions a short time later with two men.

"My name is Larem Maysen, and this is my associate, Raymon Pillath. We accept your generous offer. We were considering sending someone ahead to the city for help. It would have taken too much time, and there's no way of knowing if someone would come."

Naria stood and shouldered her packs. "We have no time to waste. Where are your sick ones? I need a bowl filled with clean water and some clean cloths," she stated and made her way swiftly to the caravan.

"We have that," a woman said and called out to another.

Doonay, Aldren, and Danarin readied themselves for a hunt. Tholan retrieved his tools from his saddlebags, glad for work. In a large tent at the Hamaros camp, Naria examined the sick ones and took the mortar and pestle from her pack to start her work, to ease the dangerous fevers. When a child vomited, she examined the matter on the ground and knew what had made them sick.

"These sick ones ate berries they didn't know were bad for them. You must find all the berries and throw them out. They mustn't be eaten," Naria explained to the group of anxious observers.

She further requested that they bring the entire lot of foodstuff they foraged from the wilderness for her to check. They didn't know what was poisonous or not and were lucky that the whole caravan hadn't died from food poisoning. She stayed in the tent and lit soothing incense until their worst symptoms of tremors, ragged breathing, and vomiting stopped. Once again, she thanked Fate for their arrival. If they had gotten there as much as half-day later, they would have come upon an entire caravan of dead and dying people.

RYLANOS

At late afternoon, Danarin, Larem, and Raymon observed the scene of the recovering camp.

"I had stopped believing in miracles, but this is one, a genuine miracle," Raymon noted.

"Our Druid would say it's fate or destiny," Danarin said.

At the lake, Naria entertained a group of children by tossing a net into the stream, then let a child hold it. They cheered when fish were caught in the net because none of them had ever caught fish before. Tholan joined them, wiping his hands with a cloth, and nodded toward the wagons. Doonay, Aldren, and two fascinated teenage boys butchered deer and rabbits.

"Those wheels should hold up the rest of the way. I put extra pegs in the supports to make them more stable. Just don't go too fast," he said with a wink.

Zora joined the men and smiled at the scene at the stream. "The sick ones look better already. Of all the things, bad berries!"

"We're sorry that some of your people died; if only we had been here sooner," Danarin said.

Naria returned with children, fish, and smiles. They danced around their parents and sang silly songs about the fish they caught. She gave a sack of fish to Zoura and left to check on the recovering patients.

After supper, Naria amused the children again with her flute. It also to practice the tune she would play over the graves of the dead for their last rites. They resumed their earlier discussion about their lives in South Peak and Port Hamaros.

"I can't imagine an entire village without the use of money," Raymor pondered.

Danarin shrugged. "We trade or do for ourselves; our people find exchanging money for food a rude practice, no offense meant."

"None was taken, although it sounds simpler," Raymor admitted.

"So, you have none who are wealthy? Or poor?" Larem asked.

"There are those who have more, but that is because they work more or don't squander what they have," Tholan added.

"I saw the difference between the wealthy and the poor in Baranos, and it doesn't look as if money has done well for either," Naria added.

"I've never met a druid, but you seem genuine," Raymor pointed out.

"I strive to be genuine, as you say. Anything else would disgrace the name of Druid, my family, and the spirits," Naria replied.

"I've never really believed in religion," Larem said.

Naria had heard that many times in Baranos. "Neither have I. Religion is what men see, which means nothing. Faith is what the Great One sees, which means everything," she said and placed a hand over her heart. "There are those who look and sound religious but have no faith. They're like empty cups, not caring if they're filled or not. I realized that when I encountered a false druid in Baranos."

Naria waited to ensure everyone finished their meals before starting the last rites.

"Before I start, I would like to know their names," she requested.

"Her name was mama," a little girl said.

A man stepped forward, picked the girl up, and hugged her. "Her mother, my wife, Laressa," he lamented.

"Be at peace; Laressa is in perfect rest," Naria consoled. "Sweet girl, can you tell me something about your mother?"

"Mama had pretty eyes and liked animals," the girl stated.

She repeated the process with each family member of the deceased, and the rites began. She lit a small candle at the foot of each grave and stood at the heads of the freshly turned ground.

"These last rites for Laressa, Adeen, Belron, and Toma are also rites for those who loved them. Death is a sad event for those left to mourn, but I would ask you to celebrate how they lived. Remember what you loved about them and keep those memories in your heart when you miss them. Death has taken them, but death cannot take away their love and memories."

She kneeled at the heads of the graves, clutched her staff close, and rested her forehead on the smooth wood. "May the Great One take their souls into the heavens, in perfect rest, until they receive their loved ones."

She chanted a language unknown to them; a gentle breeze drifted in, left flower petals on the graves, and blew out the candles. She rose and played a bittersweet tune on her flute. At the tune's end, she acknowledged the mourners and left the gravesite. The mourners nodded in respect when she walked past them, making her way to her tent.

"That was beautiful," Zora acknowledged.

"Let her know that; sometimes, she's not so sure of herself," Danarin said.

"Is she well?" Zora asked.

"Rites tire Druids. They lend some of their spirit when they perform a rite to help to guide the other spirit. It's very personal to them. Only those truly willing to give of themselves are touched to help others in this way."

*****

The following day, the companions shared breakfast with the thirty-two remaining members of the Hamaros caravan. Naria added her sweet porridge to the meal that the children enjoyed. The companions rode with the train, deciding that the city folk weren't skilled in traveling in open country. They couldn't in good conscience leave them.

"It's a wonder they made it this far," Tholan commented to Naria, who nodded in agreement.

"Last day of travel," Raymor announced.

"Larem, have you ever been to Rylanos?" Danarin asked.

He nodded and prodded a pair of oxen forward. "Last year, and it's like nothing you've ever seen. It makes towns like Baranos look like villages in comparison. You could fit ten towns the size of Baranos in Rylanos."

"Kipton, you don't have to lick the bowl, child! There's more for you!" Zora fussed, again appalled at her child's manners.

"Mind your mother, Kipton," Raymor said.

"Yes, father," the boy replied.

"If it's all right with your parents, would you like to ride on my horse today?" Naria asked the boy.

He looked hopefully to his parents, and they nodded their approval. He smiled and held out his bowl for more porridge.

Observing the caravan prepare to depart left Aldren to conclude that they were like their own little village on wheels. Naria and Tholan kept the children occupied while the caravan readied for the journey, and two hours after breakfast, they headed west once more. On Night, Kipton smiled smugly at the other children riding in one wagon. She bid Night trot to the wagon's rear and extended her arm for Garil to scamper into the wagon, and they paid no more attention to Kipton.

The closer their arrival to Rylanos, the more people they saw. It was the same as Baranos, but with twice as many people, horses, and wagons. Despite the lingering sadness of the previous day, there was a sense of excitement among the Hamaros caravan. There wasn't a sense of excitement for the companions, but cautious anticipation. The Hamaros caravan would make Rylanos their home; it would be merely another stop on their journey for the companions. When the sun set, Larem stopped and pointed to lights in the far distance.

"If you look closely, you can see the lights of Rylanos," he said.

"Why don't we have supper before going into the city?" asked Danarin.

"We'll be pleased to eat with you, but we must continue to the city and find an inn. We prefer not to sleep another night in the wilderness if we can help it. The women don't care for it, and we prefer not to hear of their concerns another night," Larem stated.

Danarin chuckled. "We understand. In that respect, we're lucky."

***

During supper, the companions listened to advice that might help them during their stay in the city.

"Visit different merchants for the same goods; haggling and bargaining is normal."

"The older merchants care more about the quality of their merchandise."

"Buy near the end of the day."

"Take care if you buy jewelry. Jalic looks the same as Quilium, and the dishonest merchants will try to fool you."

At the companion's puzzled looks, Zora explained the difference. "Quilium is prized for its use in jewelry, but I wouldn't use jalic for so much as a horse's bit."

"Metal chamber pots are usually made of jalic," Larem added.

"There is one last thing I need to mention, and that is... well, red-headed merchants flirt more than the others," Raymor said.

"I beg your pardon?" Zora asked indignantly, tossing her red hair over her shoulders.

"I'm teasing, my love," soothed Raymor.

"Perhaps we'll run across each other in the city, and we can share supper again," Larem offered and climbed into the lead wagon.

"I wish good fortune to you in the future," Danarin said.

"And I hope you're reunited sooner than later with your families. You saved our lives, so telling you that sounds inadequate."

"No, it's not; it's our deepest wish. We think about it with each step we take. May peace go with you," Naria said.

They watched the caravan drive into the distance.

"Thank goodness it's only a short distance away. They shouldn't get into too much trouble," Aldren said.

***

They ate a hearty breakfast in the morning, and Danarin made sure they looked as presentable as possible.

"We'll be speaking to a prince, so we should look our best; no need to look like a bunch of ragged barbarians," Danarin stated.

White stone walls lined the busy road toward the city, much taller than the walls of Baranos, with workers busily cleaning the walls. They worked from ground level or suspended by ropes at various heights on the wall. The companions had seen nothing like it. Unlike the dirt path into Baranos, the entry to Rylanos was paved, and workers swept and collected debris from the road. Armored sentries paced along the top of the tall walls and occasionally nodded to those that passed through the entrance. They returned a wave to Naria when she waved at them.

Two Druids meandered about an area known as the Temple Commons inside the city. They greeted others, to include a wolf-sized black night cat that flicked her tail in return.

"Good morning to you as well, Castanya. Your coat looks especially shiny this morning," one of the druids said lightly.

The night cat hissed and slinked away.

"You shouldn't tease her; those young in magic always make mistakes. The Wizard's Guild is working on a solution."

"What of Bristan?"

"Brother, I assure you there's no darkness in that young wizard. He was eager to try his growing skills, which meant no harm. When you came into your powers, you can't tell me you didn't feel like calling up a thunderstorm or two on your older brother when he teased you?"

"You're right; he meant no harm. Wizard's affairs are their own. A troublesome lot," he conceded.

"They probably think the same of us."

They paused, gripped their staves, and glanced about the area speculatively.

"Did you feel that?"

"Indeed, a druid approaches."

"A young one, much power."

They went to the nearest city gate and waited, blending into the crowd.

***

The companions marveled at the enormous towers lining the massive entry gate. Danarin met an armed sentry and inquired about the location of the prince.

"The prince, you say? You can't just walk up and start yapping at him! You must request an audience, and that's if you're lucky," the sentry stated.

"Yapping? We aren't dogs; we won't do anything of the sort!" Naria chided.

Danarin laid a hand on her arm and held up a messenger bag. "We have dispatches from the magistrate in Baranos."

"Well, that's a different kettle of fish," the sentry replied. "Wait here, I'll have someone show you to the Regent."

"What's a regent?" Tholan asked.

"He's the prince's right-hand man. All official audiences are requested through the regent."

"I understand," Danarin said.

The sentry left and returned a few minutes later with a squire. "Follow this lad, and he'll show you the way to the Regent."

The two druids watched the group's leader talk to the squire. They sensed Naria's unease at the multitude of people and the press of magic she must be feeling.

"Look at the young druid; she senses the magic. It must be new to her."

"Of course she does. Should we approach her?"

"Not yet; let us wait."

Danarin noticed a troubled look on Naria's face and the white-knuckled grip on her staff.

"Something bothers you?" he asked.

She shook her head and struggled to find the words to describe what she felt and pinched the bridge of her nose. "There's so much magical energy in this place. Some of it is strange, but powerful."

"Is it hurting you?" Doonay asked, looking around as if he could somehow find and stop it.

She shook her head and rested her forehead against her staff. "It's exciting, terrifying even, to feel so much power all at once."

"Can you continue?" Danarin asked, and she nodded in response.

They followed the squire while the two druids followed at a discrete distance. They arrived in front of a building teeming with people going about their daily business. Some spared second glances at the bigger men, obviously from the plains.

"Regent's Hall," the squire intoned with a bow and left.

"Wait here; I'll go in. No need for all of us to add more to the crowd," Danarin said and approached the large double doors of the building.

"I agree," added Aldren.

They all felt claustrophobic in the large, noisy crowd of people, and saw the doors closed behind the elder.

"What's that smell?" inquired Doonay.

"A smell like the hind end of a cow?" Aldren rejoined.

"In town?" Doonay replied. "Got any elppa left?"

"No, you ate them all," Aldren replied.

Naria turned away from their banter and looked about the crowd of people with a sigh. She tried to shrug off the unfamiliar feel of potent magical energy pressing against her from all sides. When she confronted the former druid in Baranos, he was powerless, so he wasn't much of a challenge. How would she deal with the sheer amount of power she felt from this place? Again, she keenly felt the absence of her father.

Life in the Big City

Naria sat on the top step of the regent's portico, pulled her shawl over her head, and removed her book from her pack. When Tholan sat beside her with an elppa, a small, bedraggled girl walked up to him and stared at the fruit with wide eyes. He took another from his pack and gave it to her. She ran away and returned minutes later with four more children. Tholan sighed and gave them the rest of his elppa and his bread. The children squealed in glee and ran away with the food.

"Seeing hungry children hurts my heart, and that was five of them," she said wearily.

"Look at how many there are in this city; we do what we can," sympathized Tholan.

"Doonay, annent'a, stu'uru."

"Cadmil'a, stu'uru, Aldren."

"That was good, you sound better," Naria said over her shoulder.

Doonay and Aldren continued their greetings in the old language when they were shocked by ringing bells and loud voices on the street. Two men in long brown robes were walking, ringing bells, and bellowing, "OFFERINGS FOR THE POOR! HUNGRY CHILDREN! HEALING FOR THE POOR! OFFERINGS FOR THE POOR!"

"What offerings? What is this?" Doonay asked while Aldren searched his pack for something to give.

People nearby dropped coins into a cup one of the bellowing men held. Naria reached into the pouch at her waist and withdrew a handful of gold coins for Tholan to take to the cup. Doonay gave them the rest of his bread, and Aldren dropped a few gems into a cup.

"Bless you, young man," one of the brown-robed men said, and the two continued their walking and bell ringing.

***

Inside the hall, Danarin waited for his turn with the Regent. Nine men had been in line before him, including an angry one that was escorted from the hall by guards. The door to the Regent's office opened and the guard holding the door barked out, "Next!"

Danarin rose from his seat and nodded to the guard as he passed. He stopped in front of the Regent's desk and waited. The Regent was a tall man (though not as tall as him) in his mid-thirties, stocky, with black hair and the most striking blue eyes Danarin had ever seen. As he scribbled on parchment and without looking up, the Regent made a gesture with his hand that prompted Danarin to speak.

"Good morning, Regent. I'm Danarin, an elder of the South Peak people. I come with dispatches from the magistrate of Baranos."

When the Regent extended his hand and finally looked up, his eyebrows rose in a moment of surprise at the size of the man standing before him.

"So, someone finally brings me official business. Very well, plainsman, let me see it."

Danarin opened the messenger bag and gave him three rolled parchments. The Regent unrolled the first two, read them, and set them aside. At the third, he raised an eyebrow and tucked the scroll into his cloak pocket.

"Return in two hours; I'm sure the prince would like to hear of this."

Danarin nodded. "Thank you for your time."

"Are all of your people so... robust?" the Regent asked.

"We've been told that a time or two," Danarin replied.

They jumped when the office window shattered, and a large rock rolled to a stop on the floor.

"Guards, see to that commotion!" the Regent ordered.

Danarin heard the loud, angry voices of Doonay and Aldren outside and quickly left the hall. What now?! He went out and saw Doonay holding up a man by the neck against the wall. The man's dangling feet were vainly trying to kick the larger man. Aldren held two men by their collars at the bottom of the steps, trying to squirm from his grip.

Bewildered, he called out, "What's the meaning of this? Doonay, let him down! Aldren, let them go!"

"They tried to take Naria's pack, and she's hurt!" Aldren exclaimed.

Doonay let the man fall to the ground. Aldren shoved the two away in disgust. He looked to the right and saw Tholan and two men tending to Naria. She was lying unconscious, with blood coming from a cut above her right ear.

"Lankash!" he cursed and hurried to her.

The crowd quieted when the Regent emerged from the building, a large rock in hand. "Once again, someone thought it best to throw a rock through my window," he drawled, prompting the crowd to babble and point at each other.

***

Naria's eyelids fluttered as she came back into awareness.

"Good, she's waking," a strange voice said.

She realized she was resting on something soft in a shaded, cool place. She squinted to focus on the strange faces above hers.

"He said it was juice," she mumbled.

Their lips twitched at her curious comment. "Well, she was hit on the head. Give her a moment to clear the confusion," one said.

She felt a cool cloth on her forehead and a familiar, calming scent. "Porra blooms," she again mumbled.

When she was fully aware, she looked at the two strange men. Their tunics and the marks on their arms were like her own. One gently pressed on her shoulder when she tried to sit up.

"Caton'a devit fi paral?" he asked.

"Yes, I know Druid-speak," she answered and made to sit up again.

"Not yet, young one. Your eyes are still unsettled."

"Where are my companions?" she asked.

"Meeting with the Prince. You're in Druid's Corner, in the Temple Commons."

"So, it was you I sensed you when we came into the city."

"Yes, young one. There are many with powers among us."

She again made to sit up, so they helped her to a sitting position. She clasped her hands in front of her and bowed her head.

"Honored Elders, I'm the fledgling druid Naria, daughter of the elder Druid Nidale. I'm at your service."

The two were dumbfounded at the formal, courteous greeting.

"We thank you for the courtesy, but we don't stand on ceremony here."

The other chuckled. "Indeed, none of that elder talk here. I'm simply Marden."

"And I'm Lidorn. Can you tell me of your curious comment about the juice?"

She blushed furiously. "It's quite embarrassing, brothers."

"I can assure you, young druid, that our own stories would cause your staff to dance," laughed Lidorn.

"In Baranos, I drank beer with no idea what it was. I flirted with my companions, retched on Danarin, and painfully paid for my ignorance the next morning. My companions are amused that now I sniff any drink other than water."

***

The Regent led the companions to the royal court and instructed them to stand at the rear doors until the prince summoned them forward. He was relieved to find that they were mannered, well-spoken folk. Thank the Great One! He didn't have time to give them a crash course in etiquette, as was sometimes required with uncouth court visitors. The Regent approached the throne, bowed, and gave the prince a scroll.

"Thank you, Breddock."

The prince unrolled the message and read. He glanced at the Regent, then at the four waiting at the rear doors.

"Come forward, plainsmen," he requested.

When they came before the throne and bowed, it was awkward for them. The plainsmen noted the prince was as taller than most, and his eyes were as bright green as Naria's. His hair was dark and he had no facial hair, unlike most of the men of Rylanos. He was the same age as his regent, and curiously dressed more plainly than those in the Court.

"I am Aldren Aradine, of the family Aradine, Prince of the realm of Southwilde. I understand that you're of South Peak?"

"Yes, your majesty. I'm Danarin, an elder of our people. I present Tholan, the artisan woodworker; the other two are Doonay and Aldren, two of our finest hunters."

"Your name is also Aldren?" the Prince asked, amused.

"Yes... majesty."

Prince Aldren cleared his throat and spoke. "I've read this disturbing report, but I would like to hear it in your own words."

Danarin nodded in acknowledgment and began the story with Nidale's vision. The prince rose from his seat and paced back and forth before the throne; hands clasped behind his back as Danarin spoke.

"And now you stand here," he stated when Danarin concluded the tale. "So, a group of armed ruffians is wreaking havoc on the plains? Dare they do so in my realm? If they're bold enough to do this to an entire village of hundreds of people, what's stopping them from doing it again? What's stopping them from raising a larger force? The magistrate was right about spies. They are most assuredly poking their eyes and ears about a city as large as this one."

He stopped pacing and faced the companions. "The young woman, the druid, where is she now?"

"There was a fight in front of the regent's building earlier. She was injured," reported Danarin.

The prince looked at the Regent with a single raised eyebrow. He gave off a long-suffering sigh when he responded. "There was an altercation between some thieves. Again, my window was shattered, and the young woman in question was an innocent bystander. I understand she was struck with a rock."

"Is she well?" the prince asked Danarin.

"Yes, your majesty. She's recovering in Druid's Corner; I believe it's called."

"Were the ruffians apprehended?"

"They were."

"Very well. I wish you had experienced a better welcome to our city. I'll decide on a course of action in three days' time. You'll be summoned then; where are you staying?" he asked.

"The Old Rylanos Inn, your majesty."

"Elder Danarin, I'm sorry for what happened to your village. I know you favor peaceful, but you must face a hard truth. Your people were taken by force, so are you prepared to have them recovered by force? This is a difficult question that I must consider when making my decision. With that said, I bid you a good day, hopefully better than the one you've had so far. Please give my best to the young woman. My regent will show you out."

When the companions left, the prince returned to his regent. "Breddock, give me your impression of today's events and these plainsmen."

"They appear to be forthright, proud people. Simple, yes, but intelligent. They can achieve power but don't seek it. They're uncertain of their future and fear for the fate of their families more than their own lives. They're angry that this has happened, which leaves them conflicted about a course of action, as they're a peaceful people."

The Prince nodded. "Summon my advisory council for lunch, and we'll discuss the matter."

***

When Lidorn returned with lunch for the three druids, Marden finished his examination of her staff.

"Fine staff indeed. Ah, he returns bearing food," Marden said.

Lidorn came into the room with a tray of soup, fruit, bread, and cheese. "The local magical community supports a communal dining hall. He explained that despite what the world thinks, we don't strut about with riches in our pockets," he explained.

She blushed furiously. If they only knew!

"Someone once asked me to make gold rain from the sky," Lidorn said.

"In truth, brother, that man was drunk," Marden said.

"How long have you been here?" she asked.

"Seven years. My town drove me out when our land flooded. My town blamed me for not stopping the flood."

"As for me, twelve years," Lidorn said. "Four years ago, I was ministering to a local village when I came across Marden. He joined me, and we've been here since then."

"What do you do here?" she asked.

"We work much the same as you, a go-between man and nature. Lidorn does more of the healing around these parts while I minister to the city's spiritual needs."

"Your elder told us what brought you here. We'll do whatever we can to help," Marden offered.

"I'm amazed yet concerned at what you've done so far, Naria. You've just come into your powers, but you've had to do things an experienced druid would find difficult. I assume your mentor is your father?"

She nodded sadly.

"So, you're without your parents, which is unfortunate enough for a young woman," Marden noted.

"You've also been without your druid guide," added Lidorn.

She again nodded sadly, and their hearts went out to her.

"Young one, you must have such a burden on your heart," commiserated Lidorn.

"But you handle it well. Your spirit is bright," Marden soothed and patted her hand.

Her bottom lip trembled, and she whispered. "Brothers, the burdens on my heart are so many that I can't count them. I can't bear to trouble my companions with them; they've enough of their own. My thoughts are so conflicted that sometimes I feel my powers will go beyond my control. I'm at a point where I fear my next step, my next thought."

"You've been without your mentor to help you learn a greater sense of focus; that's why you feel this way," advised Lidorn.

"What am I to do?" she asked.

"We've spent 46 and 37 years in this world and have yet to mentor a Druid. We would be honored to be that for you while you're with us," Lidorn offered.

Naria dropped her bread. "Truly? You don't know me, yet you're willing to do this? Brothers, it is I who am honored!"

***

After meeting with the prince, the companions returned to Druid's Corner in the Temple Commons. They walked along what Doonay thought looked like stables and arrived at Naria's small room. She sat on a chair beside a cot, humming and sewing on a swath of fabric. Her bedroll was on the cot, and her belongings were on a table against the opposite wall. She smiled at the group when they appeared at the doorway and put her sewing aside.

"It's good to see you well! You already look at home," smiled Danarin.

Aldren strolled in and flopped down on the cot, much too small for his long legs. She rolled her eyes at him and grasped Danarin's forearms in welcome.

"I feel much better. I'm glad you brought me here! How do you like my room?"

"It looks like a stable; the whole place does," Doonay remarked.

"Then let me bring Night here and see what she thinks! Stable indeed," she stated indignantly.

"What an astute observation," Lidorn said from behind them.

Marden looked Doonay from head to toe, and lifted an eyebrow when he spoke. "However, we find them comfortable, as does the wandering mage, druid, or priest that lives in a state of perpetual poverty."

Aldren made the sound of a cracking whip, and she smirked at Doonay, who had never been chastised so eloquently.

"You like it, which is what matters. You have a fine view of the grove, which I know you prefer," Danarin said.

"What of the hearing with the prince?" Marden asked.

"His name is Aldren. Does that amuse you?" Tholan asked.

"He's named Aldren as well? Yes, that's funny!" she said and laughed, poking Aldren in the side.

The elder druids observed the interactions of the companions. Naria appeared to care for the four, but it was clear that Doonay was a burden on her heart. Aldren was the light-hearted of the group that made her laugh the most. They could see that he was the one that kept their spirits up. Tholan, his mind always on his next project, appeared to be taking measurements of the bed and table with a knotted length of string. As for Danarin, they counted on the elder for his guidance. He was the peacemaker and voice of reason for a group of young people with varied emotions, and Naria noticeably regarded him as a father figure. Danarin left the companions to talk while walking the Temple Commons with the druids.

"I'm pleased with your offer of guidance for her," Danarin said.

"We'll do as much as we can," assured Lidorn.

"It agonized her father to know that he would be separated from her. She'll be safe?" Danarin asked.

"On my word, she will. The Temple Commons is the safest place in the city. We'll always be close by," Marden assured him.

"We're lodged at The Old Rylanos inn," Danarin informed them.

"Feel free to join us for supper in the evenings. It's usually an interesting affair in the communal hall," offered Lidorn.

Danarin returned to Naria, wished her good night, and the men returned to their lodging for the night.

***

On the way to the communal hall for supper, Lidorn and Marden explained the hall's purpose. "It's the only time all the magic users are together at one time. We have time to fellowship with those of our abilities, learn from one another, and share in each other's unique adventures and experiences," Lidorn said.

"Everyone contributes to the kitchens during the week; no one here hungers," Marden explained. "Take the mages, for example; sometimes they entertain in the city for donations and give it to the temple. They don't mind; they are mages, after all."

"He means they like to show off," Lidorn added.

"They're different from wizards who consider parlor tricks beneath them," Marden explained.

As they explained the other Temple Commons residents, she couldn't help but wonder about the fascinating intricacy of the magical social strata. How would she ever keep up? Lidorn sensed her concern.

"Don't worry; just watch and listen, you'll do fine," he said.

Watch and listen were what she did. The wizards discussed their wands, spell components, and adventures with their unique and colorful clothes. Some of them sported multicolored hair, as colorful as their clothing. The mages, less flamboyant than the wizards, distanced themselves from the others. They absently ate while reading their spell books, occasionally speaking with each other in their unique language. The monks were sociable, inquiring after everyone's well-being and singing songs in another language unknown to her. How fascinating they all were! Even a romancing couple in a far corner of the hall was sitting apart from everyone else in their own little world. They fed each other tidbits of food amidst shy, secretive smiles and whispered endearments. As hard as she tried to imagine it, she couldn't see herself and Doonay doing the same.

Meeting

The terrifying excitement she felt earlier in the day was gone, replaced with contentment and belonging. Lidorn introduced her to various folk around the hall, and it amused him how much her courtesy flattered the older ones.

"You just don't see it among the young people anymore," an elderly wizard commented and patted her shoulder.

Perplexed at the wizard's comment, she followed Lidorn to seats at a long table, and the meal began. Plates passed around the table, and the conversation started. The man beside her asked her to pass the bread, so she did. He put the bread on his plate and cleared his throat.

"Good evening, I'm Bristan. I'm required to tell you I'm a journeyman wizard on magical sanction," he said.

She chuckled. "I'm Naria, the new druid. Pleased to meet you. What's a journeyman wizard?"

"Well, there's three levels of wizardry: apprentice, journeyman, and master," he explained. "We've heard about you. Can you make it rain?"

Lidorn ate and pretended to listen to the person next to him, but listened for her answer.

"No, I can't make nature do anything; I just ask it nicely," she replied.

Bristan chuckled. "Ask it nicely? I've never heard earth magic described quite that way before."

Lidorn felt like doing a jig. This young one had it right! Mentoring her wouldn't be a chore at all! She just required a nudge in the right direction to focus on the sheer amount of raw power she held.

"Are you well?" asked Bristan.

Lidorn looked at her.

"I'm exhausted. I've had a long, strange day," she said.

He sighed and dropped his bread. "I turned my woman into a great big cat this morning. I lack the skill to reverse it, hence the sanction."

"I take it back. Your day has been stranger than mine," she admitted.

He asked more questions about earth magic, which she admitted was something she had never heard of before.

"I'm a fledgling, new to my gifts, and I'm still learning them. I've never heard of elemental spirits called earth magic," she said.

"I assume that Wizard education is more structured than Druid education, so I find myself on sanction. My master always said I needed a more structured mind. Perhaps he's right; my woman's a great big cat because of me," he mused.

"My father taught me to keep things as simple as possible. Your purpose will determine the outcome. Bad purpose, bad outcome. Good purpose, good outcome," she reasoned.

"Perhaps your father can consent to mentor me," he chuckled.

She could only imagine what her father would say about a druid mentoring a wizard. What a conversation that would be!

"Let me ask you this; did you turn your woman into a cat on purpose?"

"Yes."

"Why?"

"For fun?"

"That was your purpose? For fun?"

"I see your point. Bad purpose, bad outcome."

She laid her hand on his arm in comfort. "Fun isn't a bad thing. You're not bad; I can sense that. A mistake can be fixed and you can learn from it."

She reached for a slice of bread and noticed Marden, Lidorn, and a monk staring at her.

"Naria, are you sure you're only eighteen?" Lidorn asked.

***

The next morning, a city sentry reported to his watch commander to start his patrol.

"You have the North Wall today, Corporal Dareld. See you in ten hours," he stated, and ticked his name off a parchment.

"Yes sir," he said. *Great One, the North Wall?*

The North and West Walls lined the Temple Commons. To ordinary men such as Casden Dareld, it was the oddest place in the city. Everyone knew Temple Commons had special protection, courtesy of the local magical population.

"Turnak," he grumbled.

He ascended the North Wall stairs and turned left to meet with the sentry he was relieving.

"Mornin' Dareld, nothin' much to report. A big night cat is runnin' around the Commons, but it's an accident, so don't shoot it. Apparently, these people turn each other into night cats and such all the time," the sentry said dryly.

"A night cat magic accident?" *And so my day begins.*

The guard shrugged and held his hands up. "It's just what they told me."

"All right, go home, kiss your wife... do whatever married men do in the day."

The man wiggled his eyebrows. "Hah! This married man is trying to get his wife with child!"

Casden put on his helm and rolled his eyes. "That's more than I wanted to know, but good luck with it."

The man whistled as he descended the stairs. Casden ensured he secured his quiver to his belt and slung his bow comfortably over his shoulder. At every twenty paces, spears were mounted, and he confirmed they were secure in their mounts. He noticed a thin line of smoke from the grove at the far corner of the north and west walls. He made haste to the location in case the fire prefects were needed, but what he found when he arrived at the source of smoke changed his life forever. A young and beautiful woman dressed in a supple leather tunic was cooking (or brewing frog's eyes, perhaps) in a pot hanging over a small fire. She was also talking to a squirrel. *Well, it is the odd part of the city, after all.*

While she stirred her porridge, she heard footsteps from the walkway atop the wall above her. She looked up and held up her hand to shield her eyes from the sun glinting off his helm.

"Good morning, sir," she said brightly to the sentry.

"Morning, miss," he replied.

She picked up a book nearby and leaned against a tree to read.

"Take care you don't set fire to the grove, miss."

She chuckled and soothed the squirrel, who was now chirping furiously at him. Her lips twitched in amusement, and she looked up again, her eyes full of mirth. They were the greenest eyes he had ever seen.

"Sir, if you knew me, you would know that it would be impossible for that to happen."

What a cheeky girl! She spooned a generous helping of porridge into a bowl and resumed her reading. After her breakfast, Casden noted she left the grove and returned a short time later with two men dressed similar to her. The three sat and talked until lunch. He saw a night cat approach the three, and the older man spoke.

"I'm sorry, Castanya. We're Druid. We don't have the skill to reverse Wizard magic," he said.

The night cat walked away, sadly it seemed. A sad night cat, how about that? Perhaps today's patrol wouldn't be so bad after all. At least, it wouldn't be boring. Back and forth, he walked the circuit and returned to the grove, overhearing interesting conversations that helped pass the time.

"... but how long will she be a night cat? And why can't she transform at will?" the girl asked.

"The Master Wizard expects days at the most. Bristan tried magic too advanced for his level of skill. Like you, he needs to learn to focus his power. He perhaps chanted a syllable wrong or wiggled a finger too many times," Marden concluded flatly.

"Only experienced wizards should perform animal shifting," Lidorn added. "Druids use a unique energy. The elemental spirits grant our powers; totems are natural to us."

"Wizards draw energy from everything around them and focus it on a specific task, such as conjuring a snowball," said Marden.

They watched and waited for her to contemplate what they said. "So, if a farmer is suffering a drought and asked a wizard for help, it would be limited? A wizard could conjure buckets of water, but a druid can summon rainfall."

"Precisely, and I'm glad you mentioned totems. That's one reason your power feels erratic. Totems are part of a druid, just as much as your heart or eyes."

"My father said..." she faltered and paused, unable to continue.

"It was to be your first task after you fledged?" Lidorn asked.

"Yes," she choked and wiped a tear.

"What is his totem?" Marden asked.

"A hawk."

"Your grandfather?"

"A bear."

The two elder druids thought for a moment.

"Hmm, no consistency among the family, so there's no telling what yours will be," noted Lidorn.

"Interesting," Marden commented.

They left the grove after lunch and didn't return. Casden was disappointed that he couldn't hear more of the young woman's seemingly magical voice. *I could listen to her talk all day!* The sun was setting, and he noted the late shadow on the sundial atop the wall, so his shift would end soon. Perhaps he could find a reason to return to the Commons. He couldn't just walk into the temple and ask around for her, could he?

Master Monk, while I was patrolling atop the wall today, I heard a pretty druid talking about becoming an animal, and I wanted to ask her about it. Do you know where she is?

He kicked the wall in frustration. *Idiot!* His relief arrived and he walked home faster than usual. He had something to do!

***

Casden's father, Tyden, was once a happily married man with three young sons, but that changed when his wife died twelve years prior. The oldest son was fifteen then but was now a drunkard who would die before his time. Tyden would see no grandchildren from him. Two years younger than the first, his second son was a simple foot soldier in the Rylanos army. He had no cares or ambitions beyond his next pay packet, which he often showed. He expected to die young, so he cared for nothing. His boorish behavior often resulted in his restriction to his cohort's barracks, and he was a frequent guest in the city jail for minor crimes. He was wholly unsuitable for marriage, and no woman in her right mind would tolerate him. So, no grandchildren from that son either. His hope for the Dareld line to continue was his youngest son, twenty-one-year-old Casden. He was a promising young man but aloof, especially around women. As any father thought of a favored son, Casden was smart, kind, and good-looking enough to catch some woman's eye. He had courted women in the past, but they soon became disenchanted at the thought of being a sentry's wife. Casden's aloof nature regarding women was the result, and Tyden thought it was absurd. His son had a stable, respectable occupation that paid well enough. Casden would never be rich, but his income would comfortably support a family.

"Evening father, I brought roasted lamb for supper," Casden said and held up a sack. "How was your day?"

Tyden set plates on the dining table while Casden sliced the meat. "The Royal Public Library ordered five shelves today."

"Five? The big ones?"

Tyden nodded. "We'll use oak this time, with the lighter brown stain."

"If you need help, let me know."

Tyden chuckled. "You've got your own job, son."

"All I do is walk around, which I did a lot today. They sent me to the North Wall."

"Ah, the wizard's wall. Anything strange happen?"

"Not much, but I heard an interesting conversation between a few druids."

"Oh?"

"A spell turned some woman into a night cat, and they can't reverse it. It was odd to hear these druids apologizing to a night cat for not having the skill to change her back."

"Can't say that I've ever heard talk like that."

"That's not all. One of the druids, a young woman, was cooking porridge in the grove and talking to a squirrel. When the other two joined her, she was concerned about being unable to transform into her animal."

Tyden chuckled. "Are you going back to the wall tomorrow?"

"I don't know. It was unexpected this morning."

***

That evening, Casden passed by the tavern he usually patronized and wiped his sweaty palms on his trousers. *I can't believe I'm going to Temple Commons.* He could feel his heart thumping the closer he came to the Commons. A brown-robed man emerged at the front passage lit with candles and torches and nodded to him in greeting. He took a deep breath and walked through the passage. It opened to sprawling stone paths, lush gardens, crafted marble benches, and water dancing in fountains. When he arrived at the largest fountain and stopped, an old monk appeared beside him in a plain brown robe.

"Impressive, isn't it?" the monk asked.

"Uh... yes," Casden replied.

The man raised a finger and spoke. "This fountain has a particular history. Forty years ago, you see...."

Casden tuned out the monk's rambling tale as he looked about the Commons. He felt a gentle breeze at his back and heard a voice, her voice. He stilled and waited until she passed him before he turned to look. Her hair and hips swayed as she walked toward a building beyond the fountain. He heard her greet a night cat that exited the building. The cat m-rowed and rubbed its feline head against her thigh. She entered the building, and the monk still blathered about the fountain.

Minutes later, Naria emerged from the building with chunks of cheese on a cloth. She saw a young man looking out of place next to the Wizard Memorial fountain, keeping reluctant company with Brother Fennet. *Isn't he that sentry from this morning? Why in the world is he here? Is he lost?* She stopped next to him, watched the water dance in the fountain, and leaned toward him slightly. His nose flared at the light floral scent that emanated from her person.

"Is he still talking about the fountain?" she whispered.

His thundering heart skipped a beat. *What do I say?*

"Yes," he whispered.

She stepped away from him and spoke to the monk. "Brother Fennet, there's still some meat pie in the hall."

"Oh? In that case..." the monk said and excused himself.

When the monk was out of sight, she fully faced him. "You're the sentry from the wall this morning, aren't you?"

Cheesy Conversation

He could finally look her in the face, only to realize that he was tongue-tied at the pretty sight before him. Her bright green eyes waited for him to speak, and he found himself drawn to her full pink lips, ready to reply to him.

She inhaled, and her nostrils flared in response to an appealing scent from him she couldn't quite place. He was taller than her but still shorter than Doonay, with a stocky build. With his clothing, dark yellow hair, blue eyes, and facial hair, he differed vastly from the men in her village; yet she found she liked the difference.

"Yes, I'm a sentry."

"Well, he talks," she remarked, grinning.

Is she teasing me? He couldn't recall that a woman ever teased him, and glanced at the bundle in her hands.

"Do you like cheese?" he blurted out.

She bit her bottom lip, not knowing what quite to say. *Do I like cheese?* She thought he was the shyest man she had ever met and that he asked the most amusing question she had ever heard. *Maybe he's genuinely curious, and maybe I'm being too forward.*

"Yes, I like cheese," she replied.

"I'll bring you cheese if you wish it. There's a market with good cheese by my home," he offered.

"Um... thank you?" *I think.*

"What's your name?" she asked.

"C-Casden. Yours?"

"I'm Naria. Good night, C-Casden. Thank you for the offer of cheese," she said and walked away.

"At least it's not a spoon," she murmured.

***

He left Temple Commons, wondering what had happened. *I asked a beautiful woman if she liked cheese; that's what happened.* He wanted to tear his hair out. *I'm indeed an idiot.*

As she walked back to her room, a shift in thought caused her to come to such a sudden stop that a chunk of cheese she was holding fell to the ground. She recalled the flashes of visions during her vision quest.

In a vision, she saw her village burning, and it happened.

She was throwing a net into a lake surrounded by children, and it happened.

She saw tall, white stone walls, and here she was in a city with the same tall, white stone walls.

She saw herself talking to a young man with fair hair and had just spoken to a young man with the same fair hair.

She flinched when Lidorn placed a hand on her shoulder. "Are you well? Was it a disturbing vision?" he asked, knowing the signs of a trance all too well.

"I don't know," she said, wanting to add that the young man didn't disturb her. Rather, she was interested in him.

Lidorn blinked, confused. "You don't know if it was disturbing or not?"

"I want my mother," she mumbled and continued to her room.

Marden joined him, and they watched her walk to her room. "What was that all about?"

"I have no idea."

***

The following day, when Casden was assigned to the North Wall, he pumped his fist triumphantly. The captain shook his head and ticked his name off the list. He hurried to the wall and saw that Naria wasn't in the grove or anywhere in sight. He sighed and continued the patrol. Two hours later, she appeared with the two druids from yesterday. All three walked toward the grove with an incense stick and chanted words unknown to him. Upon arrival, they settled down for meditation and prayer. After another hour, the men opened their eyes, but hers remained closed in meditation. She yawned and slumped to the ground. They stuck the incense in the ground next to her head and observed her slumber.

She slept soundly until she twitched her feet and sniffed at the air. Lidorn and Marden quieted and stood. She sniffed again, and before Casden's stunned eyes, her feet and hands became milky white paws. Fur sprouted from her body and she fully transformed into a white and gray wolf in seconds. When she woke and rose on four wobbly legs, it startled Casden so much that he tripped over his feet and fell on his rear. He scrambled to his feet when he heard a panicked howl and saw her race across the grounds toward the commons.

"That was fast for her first shift," marveled Lidorn.

"Indeed," Marden agreed.

***

After breakfast, Danarin and Aldren walked into the Temple Commons to see Naria. Doonay and Tholan were at the inn, sleeping off their discovery of wine.

"I warned them after the second glass," Danarin said, knowing they would learn a powerful lesson when they woke.

They passed a large, ornate fountain and heard yapping and howling nearby. A wolf streaked from around the back corner of the temple and ran straight for them. Others milling about the Commons paused whatever they were doing and pointed at the crazed wolf. Wands appeared out of cloaks, and monks hurried from the temple with lengths of rope. Danarin and Aldren looked at each other in alarm. They had no weapons in hand, and a crazed wolf was heading straight for them! Casden ran atop the wall and watched the scene, hoping no one would hurt the wolf. She looked and sounded crazed, but he supposed he would be too if that happened to him. The wolf slowed when it approached Danarin and Aldren. It was the most forlorn-looking creature they had ever seen, and it looked as if it was trying to bite its tail in aggravation for simply being there. The wolf whimpered pitifully at Danarin, then at Aldren. Now, feeling sorry for the poor creature, Aldren reached out. Her eyes were wide with fright; her head drooped, and her tail tucked between her legs. She dropped to the ground with a huff and put her head on her paws.

The Druids rounded the corner at a run and called out, "Don't hurt her! It's Naria!"

Danarin and Aldren regarded her, astonished.

"Naria? I don't believe it," Aldren whispered and crouched down.

She wagged her tail and licked his hand when he reached out to her. The Druids arrived and greeted them.

"When druids first shift, most are frightened," Lidorn informed them. "She did it more quickly than most. There is much power within her."

"You can talk to her. She'll understand you," Marden said.

"She's a pretty wolf, still with her green eyes," Danarin said to make her feel better.

Lidorn kneeled in front of her and spoke. "Naria, think about the person you are. Think about walking on your two legs and eating with your hands. Think about the young man that visited last night."

"What young man?" chorused Danarin and Aldren.

She cocked her head sideways and wagged her tail. Seconds later, Naria was again before them. She swayed against Danarin and closed her eyes until the dizziness subsided.

"That happens at first," Lidorn said, feeling like a proud father. "You did well, better than we expected."

"How did it feel?" Danarin asked.

"Terrifying at first. I saw the paws, then the tail, and felt all the teeth, and all I could think was to run. When I saw you two coming into the commons, I felt like I needed to run to you."

"You recognized them as members of your pack," Marden teased.

"What young man visited you last night? That was fast, we've only been here for two days!" Aldren teased.

She did look rather fetching, with her eyes dancing and her cheeks glowing pink with excitement.

"Very funny," she retorted, exasperated. Oh well, they would find out anyway.

"Do you see that sentry on the wall, over my left shoulder? Don't look! He came to see me last night."

She left out the cheesy conversation. That memory would be hers alone when she needed something to smile about.

After Casden finished his lunch sack and continued his patrol, he laughed at the sight in the grove. Naria was a wolf again, rolling around in the deep grass, sniffing and nudging dirt and weeds with her snout. She stopped, sniffed the air, and yapped at him. It made him laugh again. At that moment, a bear loped across the grounds toward the grove. The wolf stood, her head lowered, teeth bared, ears forward, and growling; she warned she would be a formidable opponent. The bear stopped and let out a muted roar. Curious, she cocked her head when a rabbit joined the bear. Naria wagged her tail and yapped. The bear huffed and lay on its side, so she padded across the grove and joined them. She sat straight, front paws together, tail wrapped closely and neatly around her. Even as a wolf, she could have good manners.

***

After his shift, Casden stopped at a market and bought an entire wheel of cheese. When he walked in, his father set soup and bread at the dining table.

"Good, we can have cheese with supper," Tyden remarked.

Casden stopped and looked at the cheese wheel. "This isn't for us, but I can fetch some more."

"Never mind, just a thought. Who's the cheese for?"

"A woman."

Tyden's eyebrows went up. "You're bringing a woman cheese?"

"She said she liked cheese."

Tyden laughed and slapped the table. "And here I thought flowers and jewelry would do the trick!"

"Father! It's not a laughing matter!"

"Forgive me, son, but it's been a while since I've had a good laugh."

"I'm glad I amuse you."

Tyden sighed and smiled fondly at his son. "Bring the cheese. She'll appreciate the effort, but bring flowers too."

"Good idea."

"Well, son, I try every once in a while."

***

Flowers and cheese in hand, Casden walked through the candle-lit Commons passageway. At a fountain, Naria sat on a bench playing her flute. She smiled when she saw him and played a few cheerful tones to welcome his arrival. She put the flute down and stood when he approached.

"Good evening, Naria. Did I say it right? I heard your friends shout it this afternoon."

She sat and patted the bench space next to her. She liked his kind voice that matched his kind eyes and shy smile.

"Here, I hope you like it," he said, giving her the cheese and flowers.

He brought me cheese! The entire amount of it would last her a month.

"It's been a while since I've seen alenyas. They're pretty, thank you," she said of the flowers.

"And this cheese, there's so much of it!" she exclaimed and weighed the wheel in her hands.

"What were you playing?" he asked and picked up the flute.

He felt more at ease now. Naria was easy to talk to, thank the heavens, and her presence was calming.

"A song I played today at the or-pha-nage... did I say that right? Lidorn and Marden bring the children sweets, toys, and clothes every month. We healed the sick ones as best we could, and they liked the music."

He nodded in approval. "Once a year, all the sentries donate a portion of their pay packet and pool it together as one big donation to the orphanage. Many sentries grew up there, so they naturally support it."

"I love the children, but it's hard to see them in that situation. In my village, there's no such thing as an orphanage. There's always a home for those without families, always."

"Why don't you tell me about your home?" he asked.

"Are you sure you want to hear it? It's not a cheerful story these days," she said and told him of her life in the village and her vision quest.

"Coming into my powers was beyond anything I've ever felt," she said and grew sad as the tale continued.

She told of the horror of finding the village destroyed and the unbearable fear about the fate of their loved ones.

"... and that's why we're here. The prince will decide on whether he will help."

She quickly wiped away a tear that fell.

"Please don't cry; I can't bear it," he said, wishing he had a handkerchief.

"C-Casden—" she said, and he held up a hand.

"It's just Casden. I stuttered when I told you my name last night. I was nervous."

"Nervous? Why?" she asked.

She doesn't know how stunning she is, does she?

"Not because of me! I'm just me. I say stupid things, I'm clumsy, and there are so many pretty, colorful women in this city—"

He scoffed as she downplayed herself.

"I talk to a squirrel, I can turn into a wolf, and I like cheese too much!" she declared.

The only thing he could do was laugh. Her innocent honesty was enchanting. He had met no one like her.

"You have a good laugh," she smiled and reached to move a lock of hair off his forehead.

He closed his eyes when her fingertips touched his forehead, more enchanted by her gentle touch and the pleasing fragrance of her skin. His heart skipped a beat when she rested her hand on his cheek.

***

Doonay strolled toward the Temple Commons with a gift in hand that would make up for the spoon. She liked flowers *and* books now, so a flower book seemed like a fine gift. He walked through the passage and froze when he saw the pair on the bench. Naria was alone with a man and had just touched him. He knew he wasn't the smartest man on the continent, but he knew the difference between a friendly touch and what she was doing. The yellow-haired man took the small hand on his cheek, and Doonay's heart fell to his stomach. He knew how soft her skin felt, and another man was feeling that touch. Another man was looking into her pretty eyes. Doonay's heart always warmed when she sent one of her sweet smiles his way, and now this other man was receiving a sweet smile from her. He felt a distinct sadness, different from missing their families. He realized his eyes felt wet, so he wiped his eyes and looked at the wetness on his hands. *This is what crying feels like.*

The Prisoner

The following day, Naria ate a bowl of porridge in her room, humming the tune she played on her flute when Casden visited her the night before. Danarin came into her room.

"Would you like some porridge? I think I made too much," she offered.

"The prince summoned us, no time for it," he urged.

"This is sooner than expected," she said.

She grabbed her shawl and staff and left with him. From his position on the wall, Casden saw Danarin and Naria quickly leave the Commons. They met with the other companions and went to Regent's Hall, where Breddock waited to usher them through the doors.

"We beg your pardon if your breakfast was disturbed, but matters have changed quickly."

Two guards opened the doors to the court, and the companions walked through. The prince waved them forward without another word. The men bowed, and she curtsied.

"Good morrow, plainsmen, and the young miss as well. We must skip the pleasantries this morning, as there is something you must see."

He nodded at the side door. Two soldiers brought in a shackled, bedraggled man. Naria saw him and felt her heart race when she took in the green shirt, brown trousers, and brown boots.

Tholan withdrew his knife from his belt and hissed, "Devil!"

The prisoner looked just as surprised to see them as they were of him. Naria, consumed by more rage than she had ever felt, with a battle cry worthy of the finest warrior, brandished her staff and rushed toward the prisoner. Her outburst shocked the entire court, with her companions being the most surprised. Doonay scrambled to wrap his arms around her to restrain her. She fought like a wildcat in his grasp, screeching for him to let her go. He felt her staff hit his head and found that he was no longer holding Naria. A snarling, enraged wolf was at his feet, ready to spring at the prisoner in her place. He hopped back, speechless at the sight. The doors to the court burst open, and Lidorn rushed in with agitated guards and officials in his wake.

"Naria, stop!" he bellowed.

The prince held his hands up and called out, "Do nothing! The only one in danger is the prisoner!"

"Put me back in thuh lock up, please!" the prisoner begged.

He would rather someone just run him through with a sword and get it over with, than be torn apart by an enraged wolf. Lidorn approached the wolf, hands out and talking calmly.

"Naria, come back to yourself. You don't want to do this. It will stain your soul, the brightest soul I've ever met."

She didn't back down, and he had no choice. He shifted into a bear and stood between the wolf and the prisoner, stunning everyone present. There was no anger or judgment, only compassion in the bear's warm brown eyes. The wolf stepped back, looked at her companions, and whimpered. Seconds quietly passed, and Naria stood before them again. She pulled her shawl over her bowed head and stepped away from the group, and the bear returned to man form.

"I would not have stopped you, druid. This is a justice owed to you," the Prince stated.

Head still bowed; she spoke. "Sire, there's a difference between vengeance and justice. I'm ashamed to say that I forgot the difference."

He stood before her and gently lifted her chin. "Wise words, young Druid. However, this man and his rabble have now brought my justice upon them. It is a heavy burden, but necessary."

He stood once more before the throne. "Upon questioning this thing that deserted the ranks of his fellows, we have learned that your people live."

Danarin caught her as her knees buckled, and the Prince continued. "A man, the name matters not, has declared himself a governor of the Eastern Territory. There's no such region in Southwilde called the Eastern Territory, and I have named no one in the realm a governor of anything."

He shook his head at the absurdity and continued. "This pretend, self-appointed governor has also raised an armed rabble, five hundred or so of this ilk," he said, gesturing absently at the prisoner. "If this man represents the caliber of this so-called army, then our task will not be difficult."

The prince stood before the man and nudged him with his foot. "Prisoner, tell this man," he said and pointed to Doonay, the biggest man in the room, "what the pretend governor plans for his people."

Doonay's glare made the prisoner's raspy voice shake. "The guv'ner ordered thuh commander to take 'em back to thuh village with thuh army. He wants 'em to mine them jules in thuh dirt."

"He wants our people to drudge for colored rocks?" Tholan demanded.

The prince faced the hall and spoke again. "There never has, nor will there ever be, slavery in the realm of Southwilde. This absurd, self-appointed governor and his rabble have forced my hand. I decree seven days from now, soldiers of my army will leave this city and journey to liberate the people of South Peak. My Regent will demand the unconditional surrender of this pretend army to be taken into custody to answer for crimes. We will then tend to the matter of this dubious governor. What say you, Regent?"

"Aye!"

"What say you, General?"

"Aye!"

When the court concluded, Naria rushed out ahead of everyone. Danarin called out to her, but she was already outside the door. People looked curiously at the sunny sky when they heard wall-shaking thunder.

***

In her room, she packed her belongings and furled her bedroll. As she wondered what to do about the cheese wheel, she heard Danarin from the door.

"Are you going somewhere?"

"Yes."

"Would you care to tell me? That way, I'll know what to tell your father?"

She faced him. "I don't know where I'm going, oh wise elder! As for father, tell him I tried, but I went mad and failed!"

"Failed what?"

"I brought shame to the name of druid! I will seek forgiveness from the spirits for my falsehood! You deserve better!"

The thunder rumbled louder.

"That's a ridiculous notion," Lidorn chided when he appeared. "No one judges you; no one blames you."

"How can you say that? My judgment fled when I needed it most!"

Marden implored, "Because we see the goodness in you that can't be measured."

"How can you doubt yourself?" Danarin asked. "We don't doubt you!"

She started to speak, but threw her hands up in frustration and turned away from them. She covered her face, ashamed that she was breaking down in front of them. Again, overwhelmed by confusion and anger, a thunderstorm raged as she fell apart in Danarin's arms.

***

That evening, flowers in hand, Casden went to the Commons and waited on the bench as the night before. Danarin rounded the corner of the residence building and saw him.

"You're that sentry, aren't you?" he asked.

Casden rose and extended his hand. "Yes sir. Casden Dareld."

Danarin clasped his forearm in return. "She's in no state to see anyone tonight."

"I'm sorry to hear that. Can I call upon her tomorrow?"

"That'll be up to her."

***

Casden had the next day free of work, so he gobbled down breakfast and went to the Temple Commons again. He waited on what he now thought of as their bench, watching the comings and goings of the Temple Commons residents. No one asked him to leave; no strange things were happening, and people greeted him warmly. *These people aren't as odd as I thought, least of all Naria.*

"Casden?"

He stood and turned to face her. The sight of her smiling face brought a smile to his.

"It's good to see you," she said.

"Today's my day off. Have you had a good tour of the city?"

"No, I've been here most of the time, and I'll be here the next week. We'll be leaving with the army in seven days."

"A dark day indeed, so may I have the pleasure of your company today?" he asked.

"I'll just let Lidorn know," she said.

Lidorn wholeheartedly agreed that she should have a day of fun as a young woman on a young man's arm. Casden was ecstatic. An entire day with her!

"How are you feeling? Your elder told me you weren't feeling well."

There were no words to describe her emotions the previous day, and she hoped never to feel so bereft again.

"I'm better. Meditation followed by a good night's sleep made all the difference."

"What would you like to see first?" he asked.

"A place with books?"

"Very well, a place with books it is."

***

She was astounded at the uncountable number of books in the Royal Public Library.

"People like to read many things but can't always afford to buy from booksellers. They borrow books from here for a few days and return them."

"I'm learning to read," she said proudly.

"Truly? One would never know because you're so well-spoken."

"I suppose we're well-spoken because we have to be. It's how we communicate, but I'm taking it further. Reading will be the skill I pass down."

"Pass down?"

"Every Druid should gain a new skill or craft to pass to the next druid. Reading will be mine."

"I know where to go next, the public gardens," he suggested.

She adored the gardens, as he knew she would. They stopped in a tavern for lunch, and she told him of her first and last experience with beer. He laughed himself to tears when she told him about her drunken behavior.

"Vile drink," she grumbled, her pride still smarting over the experience.

"I have a drink or two when I join my friends at a tavern, but only that. My brother is a drunkard, so I know first-hand what can happen. I have no intention of turning into him."

After lunch, they stopped in a shop where artisans shaped and colored glass into flowers, animals, and people.

"So pretty and delicate," she said and admired the figures on display. She ran her fingertips over a smoke-colored wolf and reached into her pouch to take out some coins.

"Please allow me to buy this for you," he said, smiled shyly at her lingering touch when he placed the delicate wolf in her hands.

They next stopped at a bakery where she couldn't resist a slice of fresh-baked sweet oat bread with berry filling.

"It's called nisto bread," Casden said.

"Can I buy more of it to pick up later?" she asked the baker.

"Tell me how much you want. I'll make it and deliver it," the baker said.

She told him how much she wanted for the temple dining hall that night. The baker would have to bring in an additional person to help with the order, but that wouldn't be a problem with the pending profit.

"Are your people wealthy?" Casden asked when they left the bakery.

"We have a resource that others see as great wealth," she answered.

"Now I'm curious," he said.

They stopped for tea, and she took a sip before she spoke. "The ground where we live is mingled with gems."

"Gems?"

"Sky gems, earth gems, and fire gems. We don't use money, and they have no value for us except for decoration or crafts. We've been taking them from the ground for generations," she said with a casual shrug.

"You're joking, aren't you?"

"No joke. I didn't know the value until I went to Baranos. I have this heavy pouch of coins, and I've hardly used any of it. Money is such a nuisance."

"You think money is a nuisance?"

She nodded. "In this city, there are hungry families with neighbors with enough… what are the words… pocket coin to feed that hungry family for a week. Because of greed over a bunch of colored rocks, an army must rescue my people. Armies mean battle, and people die in battle. Now can you see why I think money is a nuisance?"

He nodded in agreement. "I see what you mean."

After tea, they stopped at the carpenter's shop, where she saw small, carved wooden figures in the front window. She pointed out a bear and a rabbit and knew she had to have them. He didn't tell her it was his father's shop.

"I'll buy these; they're for my friends," she said.

They next went to the stables, admired the horses for sale, then to the ranch where her pony sheltered. Night saw her at the fence and ambled toward her.

"Night, this is Casden."

The filly whinnied and pawed the ground.

"I thought as a druid you wouldn't like the idea of riding a horse or eating meat."

"There are a few flavors of druid, as my father would say. We recognize that everything in the world has a purpose. Horses are a great help to us and make wonderful companions. It would have taken us twice as long to get here without the horses, delaying the rescue of our families."

Night whinnied in agreement.

"The purpose of some animals is for food. There are places and seasons on the plains where there is no fruit on trees or food growing from the ground, so we must hunt or starve. The spirits know this. We only hunt for what we need."

"What are the other kinds of druids?" he asked.

"There are those who shun people and live their entire lives in the wilderness, serving the needs of nature. There's nothing wrong with that, it's just not a life I'd want. The Druids of my people serve both man and nature, helping people learn the value of nature while protecting it. My healing is nature-based because it's the most powerful. The poor often turn to us because we don't require payment for our services."

She told him of the insect bite sickness, the poisoned caravan they encountered, the sick and injured children in the orphanage, and one of the temple monks who recently suffered a food allergy.

"You would say you are a druid who serves both man and nature? A protector of both?" he asked.

"Good, you understand. One day, I hope to add to my duties."

"What other duties?"

"Wife and mother."

Jezzine

Naria invited Casden to supper at the dining hall, but he worried he wouldn't be welcome.

"Of course, you'll be welcome. The hall is open to all living in and passing through the city."

"Would it please you?" he asked.

She nodded. "I can spend more time with you."

How could he turn that down? He went home to tell his father that he would be out for supper. It was a good thing he planned to be elsewhere because his boorish brother was at home. Payday wasn't for three days, and he probably didn't have two coppers to rub together. He realized it was an excellent example of why Naria regarded money as a nuisance.

"Hah, got some pretty piece for the night?" his brother teased nastily.

"At least I'm not looking at other smelly men in a barracks all night," Casden replied and flipped him a single gold coin. "Eat somewhere else; I'm sure father would prefer it. You're stinking up the place."

He left the house, smirking at his brother's outraged ranting. When he entered the Commons passage, he heard Naria playing her flute. When she saw him, she stood from where she sat on a bench near the passage. She took him by the hand to lead him into the hall, gesturing to the sign above the doorway that read **Open To All**. She pointed out the prominent wizards, mages, priests, and monks and greeted a man her age who was juggling three glowing balls. She skipped a seat from him when she sat, and Casden noted others did the same.

"He's a good wizard, but clumsy, and I'm not sure what he's juggling," she informed him quietly.

"Why is he doing it at the table?" he asked.

She shrugged and passed him the bread. "Feen li ved feen li."

"Which means what?" he asked.

"He is what he is," she answered.

Bristan caught her eye and waved, heedless of the glowing balls. She winced when a ball hit him in the temple. He snapped his fingers, and the balls disappeared.

He smiled shyly and said, "purpose."

She replied with, "outcome."

"What was that all about?" Casden asked.

She passed him the bread. "A talk we had earlier this week."

***

Casden patted his stomach when they left the hall. "My belly is full. That was a fine supper. Thank you for inviting me," he said.

"You're welcome," she replied. "Would you like to walk around the square? Many do after supper. The wizards put on a show when they light the torches along the paths."

They stood among a crowd as four wizards faced each direction to light the torches. The wizard facing north pointed a wand in the air, and a ball of fire shot from the tip into the air. When it reached the height of the tallest watchtowers, it exploded into dozens of smaller fireballs that dropped to settle on the northern path's torches.

The southern-facing wizard acted as if he were shooting a bow and released a fireball from his wand that flew fast across the tops of the torches, lighting each as it went. In seconds, it was over.

One of the oldest men Casden had ever seen, the wizard facing east, removed the first torch from the ground and blew a gentle breath on it. It flared to life, and he summoned his apprentice to give him the torch.

"I'm too old to go gallivantin' around the square, walk along the path and light the torches," he instructed.

"Yes, master," the young wizard said.

The crowd roared with laughter and patted the old wizard on the back. The wizard facing the west path thought for a moment and turned to Naria.

"Care to do the honors, young druid?"

She clasped her hands in front of her and nodded respectfully. Staff in one hand, she stood at the first torch. She closed her eyes and clenched her free hand into a fist. Her eyes glowed and she opened her hand. A little ball of fire was resting in her palm.

"It doesn't burn her!" Casden whispered excitedly to the monk next to him. "Look at her eyes!"

She opened her glowing eyes, held the fireball close to her chest, and whispered. She extended her hand and the fireball hopped from her hand to the first torch. She pointed at the second torch, and it sprang to it. The fireball understood what she wanted and merrily bounced down the line of torches. The glow faded from her eyes, and she gave a small curtsy when the crowd clapped in appreciation. Casden stepped forward to examine her hand and saw that she was unburned.

"That fire understood what you wanted," Casden said, astonished.

"It's like I said, all you have to do is ask nicely," she said.

"Would that work for a kiss, perhaps?" he asked and braced himself for a slap that might come from being so forward with such a stupidly-posed question.

He stepped closer and took her hands in his. "Beautiful Naria, may I have a kiss?"

"Yes, you may," she smiled.

He drew her closer, cupped her chin, and pressed his lips to hers.

"Good show, lad," the elderly wizard quipped as he walked away.

Naria grinned, agreeing with the old wizard's comment. She wasn't an expert on romance and such (she had kissed only one person a few times in her brief life), but she knew what was happening with Casden was special. She knew she could stand there all night and kiss him and not tire of it.

Her companions watched the light show from the balcony of their inn and clapped when they saw her torch-lighting antics; however, her next antics would prove more surprising. They watched as she and a man known to them as "Casden the sentry" came together for a kiss.

"After only three days in this city, and she's already kissing on someone! Not as much as one woman has looked my way!" Aldren exclaimed in mock indignation. "And just how long is that kiss going to last, I ask you? All night?"

Danarin felt Tholan nudge him in the side and nod toward Doonay, watching the kissing scene with anguished eyes. He gave Doonay a consoling pat on the back when he noticed the young man's hands gripping the balcony railing so hard that he thought the wood might crack.

***

Before leaving for his shift the following day, Casden let his father know he wanted to invite Naria and Danarin for supper that night.

"Who's this Danarin fellow?" Tyden asked.

"From what she told me, he's an elder of their people, acting in place of her father and guiding the men."

"Hmm, sounds all right. It's been a while since we had company for supper," Tyden said.

He reported for his shift and surprised the captain when he requested to stay on the northwest patrol. "This is unexpected. You have rank over many of the sentries of your shift; you can return to the eastern sector if you wish. Any reason for the sudden change of heart?"

"Respectfully, sir, the reasons are my own."

"Fair enough; I'm glad I found someone willing for the patrol. Congratulations, you're now the northwest patrol leader."

***

Naria's eyes fluttered open, and she became aware of Garil's chittering and an unfamiliar woman's voice. She pushed the hair from her face and looked up. A woman who looked to be her age leaned on the open windowsill, cooing at Garil. She caught Naria's eye and patted her feet.

"Good morning!" she said cheerily.

"Morning," Naria tiredly replied.

"It's so good to have another woman my age around here to talk to. I'm Jezzine Dranesta. Yes, I know, it's a mouthful."

"I'm Naria of South Peak. Pleased to meet you. What's a mouthful?"

"Would you like to go to breakfast?" Jezzine asked.

After just five minutes, Naria was reminded of Rillorna, twenty years younger. Jezzine was just as friendly and clamorous as the older woman, which made her smile. Her conversation bounced from one topic to another at lightning speed, laced with amusing observations that reminded her of Aldren. At breakfast, she learned Jezzine was a twenty-year-old mage originally from Port Hamaros. While Jezzine explained she had recently completed her apprenticeship with her master in Rylanos, Naria still wondered what Jezzine's 'mouthful' comment meant.

"This was his mastery gifting to me," Jezzine said and held up a necklace with a pendant made of a glimmering stone. "A Quilium chain adorned with the stone of my birth."

"Stone of your birth?" Naria asked.

"You didn't get out of South Peak much, did you?"

"Admittedly, no."

"Well, I was born in the seventh month, and the stone of the seventh month is Ranasta," Jezzine explained.

"I understand."

"What month were you born in?"

"This month."

Jezzine searched through the objects in her pouch and held a glimmering green stone for Naria to examine.

"The sixth month is a Naria stone. I should've connected it with your name. You can keep that," Jezzine offered.

"Thank you."

"So, do you have a man yet?" Jezzine asked.

Naria choked on her milk at the sudden personal question.

"I'll take that as a yes," Jezzine said, leisurely buttering her bread until Bristan and Castanya, back to womanly form, walked in.

Jezzine stiffened, leaned close, and spoke. "Bristan was courting me until Castanya came along, and then poof! No more Jezzine. I don't know what he sees in her."

Naria tried not to laugh at the blatantly jealous comment.

"No matter, you can't put the spell back in the wand, as my master says," Jezzine conceded.

When a sentry messenger entered the hall and removed his helm, a monk approached him. "Have you eaten this morning, young sir?"

"Thank you, but my mother made a fine breakfast. I have a message for the Druid Naria."

Everyone stopped what they were doing and looked at her. That rarely happened in their part of the city. An official message arrived for one of them during breakfast?

"I'll take it to her," the monk said and delivered the message to her.

Naria thanked him and unrolled the parchment with a sigh. "I'm just learning to read; it'll take me half the day. Can you read it for me?" she asked Jezzine.

While breakfast chat continued throughout the hall, and Jezzine read the parchment with a chuckle. "It seems your gentleman friend missed seeing you this morning about the grounds. He invites you and your elder to supper this evening at his home. He also wants to tell you how much he enjoyed last night, and plans to ask nicely again."

She primly re-rolled the message and gave it back to Naria. "It's always the quiet ones," she commented and looked sideways at Naria, patting her heated cheeks.

"Good heavens, just what did you two do?"

"We kissed, that's all."

Jezzine raised a single eyebrow.

"A kiss, that's all!" Naria declared.

She saw that Jezzine, Lidorn, Marden, Bristan, and Castanya looked at her with curiously amused expressions to her damaged sense of discretion. She could only imagine the humor her father would have seen in the situation.

"Must have been some kiss," Jezzine quipped.

***

After breakfast, Jezzine went with Naria to let Danarin know of the supper invitation. In front of The Old Rylanos Inn, Jezzine stopped.

"Your companions stay here?" she asked, bewildered. Only the wealthy lodged at The Old Rylanos Inn.

"Yes, is something wrong with it?" Naria asked.

"Are you rich?"

Naria rolled her eyes and opened the door. How many times was she asked that? "Not exactly."

The plainsmen in the dining room stood when the two women approached.

"Great merciful heavens," Jezzine muttered as they made their way to the men's table, wondering why Naria would romance a sentry when men like this were readily available. *There's an entire village of them?!*

"Good morning, plainsmen. May I present the mage Jezzine Dranesta, presently of Rylanos," Naria said.

They put a hand over their hearts and nodded in greeting. *How charming!* Jezzine thought.

"Jezzine, I proudly introduce Elder Danarin of South Peak village. My other companions are Aldren, Tholan, and Doonay."

"Would you like to sit down?" Danarin asked.

Aldren took chairs from another table for the two, and his gaze lingered on Jezzine. His gaze didn't go unnoticed, so she decided that a touch of flirting was in order.

"Would you like something to eat?" Aldren asked and held out a platter of fruit.

"That looks good, thank you," Jezzine replied and took a slice of melon from the platter.

"But we've already—" Naria started but quieted when Jezzine's rather pointy elbow quickly nudged her. Oh.

"Some bread and juice too? Perhaps some milk?" Aldren asked.

"That would be lovely," Jezzine replied, and accidentally (or not) placed a lingered touch on Aldren's hand when she took bread from the plate.

"So Aldren serves food now?" Doonay asked under his breath, and Tholan gave him a quick kick under the table.

"Elder, Casden has invited us to his home for supper tonight," Naria said.

"I know; he came here earlier this morning and asked. I told him it would be up to you."

"Yes!" she exclaimed, and the table quieted.

Like at the dining hall, they all regarded her with amused expressions.

"I mean, yes, it was nice of him to ask," she said calmly.

Jezzine scoffed. "Oh please, you're practically ready to have his babies."

Doonay's juice sprayed from his mouth at the comment. Mortified, Naria let her forehead fall on the table with an audible thump. Tholan slapped Danarin's back to dislodge a bit of food suddenly caught in his throat. His older sisters teased each other often in such ways, so he was used to hearing such comments. Aldren, whose laughter echoed off the walls, was half in love with the outspoken, amusing mage. Naria, scandalized, wished she had magic that would allow her to just disappear.

***

Back in her room, Naria searched through her belongings for her flute. Lidorn said he was returning to the orphanage to check on some children he had treated for fevers.

"I'll join you. They like the music," Naria said.

Jezzine examined Naria's belongings and waved her wand to cast a blooming charm on a pot of wilted flowers. She saw the staff leaning in the corner and admired the carvings on the smooth wood. It was tempting to touch, but like a wizard's wand, you don't touch handle a Druid's staff. You never know what might happen.

"That's a fine staff, but it's like carrying around a tree," Jezzine remarked.

Naria grinned. "A sapling, actually, and try it when you're seven. It's not a chore anymore. It's part of me now; I can't channel power without it."

Jezzine held up a small glass wolf. Naria grinned and transformed into her wolf.

"Amazing! Can you do other animals?"

Naria shook her head and licked her paw. They heard hurried footsteps, and Lidorn appeared at her door, breathless. Naria returned to her true form.

"Come quickly. A child at the orphanage has fallen desperately ill," he urged and left as quickly as he came.

She grabbed her knapsack and staff and followed. Jezzine followed too, hoping she could help. When they arrived at the orphanage, it was too late. An eight-year-old boy had woken with a fever and vomiting and suffered a seizure. He lost consciousness soon after, and his heart gave out. He lay covered with a blanket in the orphanage matron's office.

"It happened so quickly," she said and wiped her tears with a handkerchief. "The poor lad."

Lidorn took her hands in his. "I'm sure you did everything you could, and he wasn't alone when he passed."

Naria was already at the boy's bedside, whispering a prayer. She laid her hand on his head and wiped the tears from her face. "Be at peace, little one."

"Is there anything I can do?" Jezzine asked.

"Yes, young mage, it's kind of you to offer. You can tell the keeper of the ossuary that there will be a service this afternoon," he said.

"I'll take care of it," Jezzine said and left the building.

"Lidorn, I humbly ask to perform the last rites for this child," Naria requested.

"We have no clerics currently in the city; if Marden were here, he would perform the rite. It's a great kindness for you to offer," he said.

He found she was true to her word. The residents of Temple Commons agreed she was doing an honorable deed and joined the proceedings. Many families and communities cast out them as children, fearing their abilities and viewing them as oddities of nature. Masters took in most of them to learn their craft, so they regarded their masters as their mother and father.

They might grow to be skilled practitioners of their art, but there would always be a corner of their hearts with the knowledge that at one time, they were unwanted.

She and Lidorn prepared the boy with care fit for a king and laid him in a finely adorned oak casket, vice the boxes of cheap wood used for the poor. Wizards, mages, priests, monks, and orphanage matrons lined the path leading from the Temple to the Commons passage. Jezzine carefully levitated the small casket along the way and through the passage where Naria stood with Night, ready to pull a carriage. Even the pony sensed the event's seriousness and stood still while the casket was placed in the carriage.

"Come Night, let's take this little one to his final rest," she whispered and patted the pony's neck.

Casden and the sentries on the walls respectfully removed their helms when the carriage passed in front of them.

Dinner Date

After the funeral, Naria said that she wanted to rest before supper. She excused herself from the communal hall, leaving Danarin with Lidorn and Jezzine.

"Has she performed rites before? At 18?" Jezzine asked.

Danarin nodded. "We met a stranded caravan before we arrived in Rylanos. Four of their number died just before we came upon them."

"Will she be all right? She didn't know that boy, but she took it personally."

"She reveres life, and rites tire her. She lends part of her spirit to guide the spirits of those who pass on. Only those truly willing to give of themselves are blessed to help others that way."

"I feel bad about teasing her as I did. She has such a kind soul, the kindest I've ever met," Jezzine said.

"Don't feel bad. If you angered her, she would let you know. She's slow to anger and gives as good as she gets; ask Doonay. Aldren teases her often, as does her father, so she's used to it. Make her laugh if you can."

***

In the late afternoon, Jezzine helped Naria prepare for supper at Casden's home. She wanted to look her best, so she dressed in a new tunic and shawl she had worked on for days. She picked her nicest hairband, and allowed Jezzine to apply a light mist of her most pleasing perfume. She contemplated her staff leaning in the corner and decided not to bring it.

"Not bringing your sapling?" Jezzine asked lightly.

"I can't believe I'm saying this, but I've been druid enough today, so the sapling stays here. I'm just going to enjoy a nice meal with a man I like. How do I look?"

"Hearts will break around Rylanos tonight."

Naria chuckled. "I wouldn't go that far."

Tyden watched his son pace the room and repeatedly look in the mirror, out the window, then back at the mirror.

"This must be some woman to get you in such a state."

"You'll see, father."

He went to the kitchen (again) to make sure everything was perfect. He had to make a good impression on Naria and the elder.

"Son, the fish won't jump from the pan to the platter," he heard from the parlor.

Casden heard someone knocking on the front door. He rushed from the kitchen, took a deep breath, and opened the door.

"Naria, Elder, welcome to the Dareld home," he said and gestured for them come inside.

Naria pulled back her shawl, glanced around the parlor, and nodded at Tyden.

Tyden chuckled. "Well done, son. She's a beauty."

"Master Dareld, thank you for allowing us to enjoy supper in your home," she said, blushing at the compliment.

"My, aren't you a polite one? The last one Cas brought home had some bad manners," Tyden said and showed them to seats in the parlor.

The last one Cas brought home? Casden quickly returned to the kitchen to set the table, not wanting to hear his father say anything else to embarrass him.

"This young woman has never brought me concern about her manners. Her parents raised her well," Danarin said.

"I've heard bits and pieces about what's happened to you. Since the South Peak decree, the army's put in more orders at my shop," said Tyden.

"What shop is that?" Danarin asked.

"Carpenter shop."

"Is that so? If you need extra help, let me know. One of the young men with me is a woodworker, a fine one at that. He sorely misses his work," Danarin said.

They heard glass break from the kitchen.

"All right in there?" Tyden called out.

"The table's set, but don't come in just yet," Casden said with an edge to his voice.

Tyden sighed and went to the kitchen. A minute later, he returned to the parlor and retrieved some cloth from a box under the window.

"He went and cut his hand."

Naria rose from her chair. "Is it bad?" she asked and went to the kitchen, where Casden held a cloth to his hand. "No, that won't do. Do you have a wash bin?"

"Yes, room off the back stoop," Tyden said.

She submerged his hand in the smaller bin on the countertop in the washroom. She cut a swatch from the bottom of her tunic with a knife from the kitchen, and pressed the leather to the cut.

"You must keep pressure on the wound. This leather will work well."

"You didn't have to cut up your new tunic," he said.

She wrapped the cloth tightly around his hand to hold the leather on the cut. "Keep this in place until the bleeding stops. Wash it with warm water and salt before you go to bed. If it's painful or swollen tomorrow, tell me, please?"

If she had her knapsack, the cut would be stitched, healing poultice applied, and wrapped with a kiss to make it better.

"Are you that concerned over a simple cut?" he whispered and drew her closer.

"If so much as a gnat bites you, I want to know," she replied and kissed the bandaged hand.

"I'm a lucky man; those gnats better watch themselves," he said and gently kissed her.

"Fish is gettin' cold," his father said from the kitchen.

***

Casden walked her back to Druid's Corner after supper. "I'm sorry if my father said anything awkward tonight."

"That's a curious apology. He said nothing awkward. I like him," she replied.

"Thank you, because sometimes he—"

She rested a finger on his lips to quiet him, not wanting to hear a Doonay-like comment from him.

"He is what he is, Casden. Be grateful that he's here. I'd give anything to spend just a few minutes with my father."

She stepped back and wiped her eyes. "Good night, take care returning home. Tell your father that I enjoyed supper."

She resumed the path to her room, again wiping her eyes, and he became alarmed by her sudden emotional departure. *I'm such an imbecile! I made her cry! Go after her!* He hurried after her and gently laid his hands on her shoulders, as he had seen Danarin do to calm her.

"I'm sorry for being such an imbecile; I can't bear the thought of leaving you upset," he urged and waited for her to push him away, to be told to go away.

Instead, she pulled him closer and burrowed her face into the folds of his shirt. "Then don't leave," she mumbled into the fabric.

He lowered his head to meet hers and lifted her chin. "I'm sorry. Forgive me?"

He believed in miracles once more when she nodded, and they continued to her room, their hands clasped.

"Doonay says the building looks like a stable. Do you think that?" she asked.

Casden looked at the building, his head cocked sideways to get a better look. "More like a barracks."

She slowed her steps in front of her room. "It's not much, but for now, it's home."

He noted the simple furnishings of a cot, table, chair, staff in the corner, and a second table with a small wash bin. A pack and a smaller knapsack hung on wall pegs. A lantern, vase of flowers, the little glass wolf, and a book were on the table.

"Does it bother you?" she asked.

He faced her. "Does what bother me?"

"That I'm not like other women in the city. I don't have fancy clothes, coloring on my face, pretty jewelry, I—"

His lips stopped her words. Surprise turned into pleasure when the kiss deepened, and she felt his tongue brush her lips. Oh!

He stopped and cupped her face. "Do you want fancy clothes? Jewelry? Do you want to be like them?"

She shook her head.

"*Then don't.* You're perfect the way you are! To me, right here, right now, you're the most beautiful woman in this entire blasted city!"

From her window seat across the way, Jezzine watched the endearing scene unfold while she weaved a basket. Naria was one lucky woman. A man had just told her she was the most beautiful woman in the city. *If a man said to me that, I'm not sure I'd live through it. The shock alone would kill me.*

The Proposal

Naria woke with the sunrise and looked at the simple calendar she had made. On parchment, Naria had drawn seven suns to count down their days left in the city, and she placed a mark through a sun at the end of each day. On the fifth day, a sentry in Casden's company was wedding his sweetheart, and he was going to the ceremony. He was let off shift early for the event, and he invited Naria to go with him.

"I wasn't planning to go, but I thought it would be fun for you. Besides, I've known the fellow most of my life; I should go," he said.

Naria went to the Old Rylanos Inn and greeted her companions as they ate breakfast.

"What are your plans today, busy bee?" Aldren asked.

"I know you have plans... with Jezzine," she teased, and chose a piece of bread. "A wedding is what I'm doing today."

What happened next was something she would remember as one of the most amusing moments of her life. They jumped from their chairs, protesting, while she casually took another bite of bread. Poor Danarin looked like he was going to have a heart attack. They stopped and looked at her, expecting her to say something.

"What?" she asked.

"Explain yourself!" Danarin demanded.

"Explain what? You see, a wedding is where two people—"

"This is not funny! Not one bit!" Danarin demanded. "How could you even think—"

"Me, think what? What are you raving about? I'm going to a wedding with Casden today as a guest," she said, her lips twitching with mirth.

Aldren was the first to catch on. "Naria, you shouldn't have let us go on like that! Look at our poor elder! His old heart can't handle shocks like that!"

"Cheeky girl... young people..." Danarin grumbled and left the table.

***

At the wedding that afternoon, Casden grasped Naria's hand when the groom vowed to love his bride until the breath of life left his body. She clapped and wiped her tears with the other women when the bridal couple shared a sweet kiss to seal the promise made to one another. The joy of the wedding celebration was just what her burdened heart needed. She had never danced like these people, so she watched what everyone else did and joined the fray. Casden watched her clap, hop, and sway with the others and felt his heart swell with pride when he saw other men give her praising looks. That beautiful woman was with him! When the time came to dance with a partner, his heart again thrilled when she stepped quickly into his arms.

"I take it you're enjoying the celebration?" he asked.

She nodded. "Wouldn't it be wonderful if there was a marriage celebration every day? To feel this joy every day!"

"I feel it every day that I'm with you," he admitted and brushed a stray lock of hair from her eyes.

She raised fingers to his lips and traced his lips as if they were fascinating to her.

His voice trembled when he asked, "What are you doing?"

Her lips twitched. "Learning."

"Learning what?" he asked.

"You," she answered.

Her fingertips moved along his jawline, then around his neck, while her nails lightly raked the hair that curled at the nape of his neck. No one had ever touched him like that. When she rested her face against his neck, her lips were gentle against the pulsing vein. The sensuality of her exploring actions was his undoing, and his lips melted with hers in a feverish kiss.

***

In the late afternoon, Lidorn and Marden took her outside the city to the countryside for their totem lessons.

"We'll spend the afternoon in our totems," Lidorn said.

"Good, because my human feet ache from dancing," she said.

"We'll see how long you can stay in your mind before the wolf's mind takes over. We won't let it get too far, especially if other wolves come 'round," assured Marden.

"It can be a fine opportunity for you to interact with other animals, to understand them better," added Lidorn.

She had a good time with the other animals, especially when they sensed she wasn't a wolf with a ready appetite for them. A bear and rabbit joyfully watched a wolf frolic with the animals in the countryside. When the lesson ended hours later, she took an extra-long bath, explaining that she felt dirty. Highly amused, Lidorn and Marden told her she neither smelled nor looked dirty but experienced the lingering effect of heightened canine smell. However, she wasn't taking any chances to meet with Casden smelling like a wolf that had frolicked through the countryside for hours.

***

That night, he arrived with slices of the nisto bread she enjoyed so much.

"Let's sit in the grove; you spend much time there," he suggested.

"It's one of my favorite places to be," she said and held his hand as they strolled to the grove.

"Tell me then, what's your other favored places?" he asked.

"Hmm... lakeside at my village... a warm bath... being in a comfortable bed," she said, unaware of how her admission sounded.

He chuckled. "A comfortable bed is one of your favored places? You're going to make some man happy with that."

She slowed, blushing at how her innocent comment sounded. *I keep saying things like that!* "Casden, what I mean is that I enjoy the—"

"I know what you meant, pretty one," he chuckled.

She sat and reclined against a tree, while he looked up at the wall looming over them.

"This is where I first saw you; you were cooking something that morning. I thought you might be boil frog eyeballs."

She patted the ground beside her, looking at him curiously. He sat and took one of her hands in his.

"Why would anyone boil frog eyeballs? To what purpose? Those poor frogs!" she exclaimed, her lips twitching in amusement.

"It was just a stray thought before I came to know you. Magic is strange and frightening to those who don't have the gift."

"You thought I was strange and frightening?" she asked, as a giggle escaped from her lips.

"Not anymore. Now, I think you're a beautiful, sweet woman who happens to be a druid."

"I'm glad we took a chance to know each other for who we are," she returned.

He squinted at something in the distance. "I can see why you like it here, but I don't know why those two are up a tree."

"What tree and what two?" she asked.

"See that tall tree over there by the west tower?"

She squinted to look and shook her head. "Those two would be Aldren and Jezzine. That means there could be a dozen reasons they're in the tree, with each reason more absurd than the next."

"Your elder must have his hands full with your bunch."

"Well, Aldren and I tease each other to distraction. He's like the brother I never had."

"Can I ask you something personal?" he asked.

"You may, although I may not answer."

He slid the shawl from her shoulders and ran his fingertips over the colored scars on her arm. "What are these for? Did it hurt?"

"These are marks of a Druid. No matter the flavor of the druid, we all have them. The colors are for the elements, and the three marks stand for our time in this world; birth, life, and death. I asked the spirits for blessings with each cut, and yes, it hurt. The scars remind me of pain that lasted for a little while but healed."

"Like life," he said.

She nodded. "I had to prove that I could take the pain I knew would come and move past it."

"Will your children be druid?" he asked.

"Only Fate knows that."

"You have a lot of trust in something you can't see."

"It's called faith. I don't need to see it; it's here," she said and placed her hand over her heart.

"Can I tell you something personal?" he asked.

She nodded and he placed a soft kiss on her hands. He swore he could hear his heart pounding in his chest at what he was about to tell her.

"My heart is no longer my own. It's in your hands," he said earnestly.

She almost knocked him over with the force of her sudden embrace. In her exuberance, she straddled his thighs, her body pressed against his. The intimacy was breathtaking for them both.

"I love you so very much, woman of the plains," he whispered.

Her lips tickled his ear when she whispered, "I love you too, sentry of Rylanos."

That evening, while weaving, Jezzine observed a scene of Casden returning Naria to her room with a passionate kiss. *It's always the quiet ones!* After Casden left for the evening, Jezzine paused from weaving when she saw Naria close her eyes and raise her arms to the sky in triumph.

For his part, Casden couldn't contain himself when he got home. "Father, she loves me!"

***

Naria woke with the dawn, noted the suns marked through, and felt thrilled with the previous night's memories. He loves me! Her heart full of new, exciting love, she rushed out of the room, colliding with Jezzine.

"OOF... I'm sorry, I wasn't paying attention," apologized Naria.

Jezzine chuckled. "Good heavens, look at you! Would a man have something to do with it all a-flutter and glowing?"

Naria nodded excitedly and told her of last night's events on the way to breakfast.

"And if someone asks about the little bruise on your neck, just say that...?" Jezzine queried.

"Jezzine, what are you talking about? I swear you say the oddest things."

"Fine then, let everyone think it's a love bite," she said and shrugged.

Naria sputtered an unintelligible response and put her hand to her neck.

"It's all right; we all get carried away from time to time, even sweet little druids," Jezzine teased.

***

After breakfast, Naria decided that her mind was running amok, so she set out to keep herself occupied. She aided Marden with a Season of the Sun ceremony, helped the monks tend their vegetable gardens, fetched water for the kitchens, and planted new flowers around the larger fountains. No matter how much work she did, Casden was always on her mind, but the thoughts were more of a whisper than the torrent from the morning. At lunch, she debated Bristan about the value of conjuration versus illusion when Jezzine returned.

"How was the trial?" Bristan asked.

"Amusing, the fellow was sentenced to a month in jail," Jezzine replied.

Naria wondered why a trial or jail would be amusing, but Jezzine said odd things, so she shrugged and continued her meal. She sighed and once again was lost to daydreams. Jezzine poked her arm and pointed to the door. She looked and Casden stood there, flowers in hand.

"How charming," an older woman noted and smiled at Naria.

She rose and went to him, noting the different uniform he wore. He ushered her outside and gave her a quick kiss. It was amazing to him how easily she accepted his affection.

"Good morning; I'm happy to see you. Did the sentries get new uniforms?"

"This sentry did when he joined the army."

She stepped back in surprise.

"This morning, I resigned from the sentries and joined the army; the troops that will take back your village," he said matter-of-factly.

All color drained from her face, and she gripped his blue satin tunic. "But why? You could die! You're safe here, this is your home, and I couldn't bear it if something—"

He took her face in both hands and gave her a heated kiss to silence her protests. "I don't have time to explain right now, but I'll be back as soon as possible. Everything will work out. Have faith, isn't that what you tell me?"

He winked and left the square.

***

She no longer had an appetite or felt the need for something to do. Her mind felt muddled, so she did the only thing she could think of and retired to her bed. A shadow fell over her, and she heard Jezzine's voice.

"If he hurt you, I'll make feathers grow from his head," she quipped.

"Jezzine, I don't care for jokes right now."

She went inside, moved Naria's feet aside, and sat on the end of the cot.

"Why don't you just come in?" Naria asked ruefully.

Jezzine poked the bedroll. "How can you stand to sleep on this?"

"Then do some magic to make it better!" Naria snapped. "It's my bed, not yours!"

"Would you like me to? I can make this feel like the most heavenly bed in the world."

Naria sighed. "I give up. What do you want?"

"When the kindest person I've ever known feels unkind, something must be wrong."

She sat up. "I'm sorry. I have no reason to be unkind to you."

"What happened?"

"He joined the army."

"When you say he, you mean Casden?"

Naria nodded. "He joined the army going to South Peak."

"You're angry because the man who loves you is going to fight for you? I'd take that as a compliment."

Naria grabbed her shawl. "I'm going to talk to Danarin. Are you coming?"

"No, Aldren has a surprise planned."

Knowing Aldren caused Naria to grin and quip, "Better you than me."

"Ha. Ha," Jezzine deadpanned.

***

Danarin was in the back garden of the Old Rylanos Inn with Tholan, sharpening knives and laughing about something Aldren had said.

"Good morning, my favorite flame thrower. What brings you here?" Tholan asked.

"I need counsel," she replied.

When Tholan made to leave, she rested a hand on his shoulder. "You don't have to leave. I trust you."

"I'm honored to have your trust, but counsel with elders is a private matter if we're in South Peak or not," he said kindly and left.

Naria took a seat and plucked at the hem of her tunic. Danarin sat back in his chair and cleared his throat.

"He loves you; do you know that?" he asked.

She nodded. "I love him too."

"We, meaning we men, don't take that lightly. So have faith that he knows what he's doing in his love for you," he advised.

"Do you know what he did?" she asked.

"Yes, he joined the troops going to take back our home. Any doubts I might have had about him are no more. I know you're worried, but I'd take it as a compliment."

"That's what Jezzine said."

"Well, if Jezzine the Wise said it, it must be true," he drawled, a teasing note.

She couldn't help the laughter that spilled out at the *Jezzine the Wise* comment. That would be like calling Doonay a hopeless romantic.

"Why don't you tell me of this Season of the Sun ceremony you helped with today?" he asked.

Casden didn't come to see her that night, but talking with Danarin helped. Her heart lighter, she marked another sun off the parchment.

***

The following day, after breakfast, she decided that meditation was the order of the day. She needed clarity more than ever for her flurry of thoughts. *Casden... Journey... Home... Renegades... Armies.* Staff in hand with a water skin slung over her shoulder, she headed for her corner of the grove. She was determined to stay there and meditate, no matter how long it took.

Hours later, Jezzine and Aldren watched her from the balcony of her room.

"She's been out there for hours," noted Jezzine.

"I've seen her father meditate for days at a time," Aldren said. "No food, no water, just sitting in a trance for days."

They heard footsteps and saw Casden striding toward the grove.

"I want to help her, but I don't know what to do," Jezzine fussed.

"This is something only she can sort out. You're here for her, that's what counts," Aldren assured her.

Casden stopped before her, noting her glowing eyes behind closed eyelids and her hands resting limply on her crossed legs. She looked to be barely breathing.

"Naria?" he asked softly.

Her fingers twitched, her eyelids fluttered, and then she swayed and fell flat on her face. It wasn't how she usually woke from trances. Casden swore under his breath and lifted her from the ground, cradling her in his arms. She enjoyed being in his arms and settled in his lap, allowing her eyes to focus and the pain in her head to clear.

"I'm sorry, are you all right?" he asked, plucking a leaf from her hair.

"I'm supposed to wake from meditation slowly, on my own. However, I woke in your arms, so wake me anytime," she teased.

"I still feel like a dolt; you fell on your pretty face."

"I've done worse, believe me," she chuckled.

He hugged her closer. "Tell me."

She looked at the sky and sighed. "Among my people, my nickname is falling leaf. Want to guess how I came by that name? When I was seven, I fell from a tree trying to get a piece of fruit and broke my arm."

For an hour, she ran through the litany of accidents and poor judgment calls she had experienced in her eighteen years because of her curiosity and clumsiness.

"I want to learn these things about you! I want to know everything about you, your family, your people," he said.

"What do you want to know?" she asked.

He took a deep breath and spoke. "The best way for me to do that would be to... to... be your husband."

"Are you asking me to—" she sputtered.

"I joined the army to prove to you, your family, and your people my devotion to you. I had had little regard for fate or faith until I met you, but there's a reason for everything. I know that now!"

"You do?" she asked, amazed that he had finally realized what she had always known.

"Why would fate bring you across a continent to talk to a sentry atop a wall? You're going back to your land, and I intend to follow you because my home will be wherever you are. Marry me, Naria, be my wife."

He took a Quilium chain adorned with a Naria stone pendant from his pocket. Her eyes went wide.

"Say you'll marry me. I'll be a good husband to you. I'm a carpenter's son, so I can build you a fine home on the plains, or here, or on top of a mountain, wherever you wish."

Her lips trembled at his declarations and the hopeful, loving expression on his face. "You said being in bed is a favored place? I'll craft you the finest bed on the continent," he declared as her giggles spilled out. "You also said that you love children, so we can lie about and make a dozen babies on that bed if you wish!" he declared, loving the sudden, furious blush on her cheeks.

A dozen? Great heavens! "I love children, but two or three is enough for anyone," she returned, fiercely blushing at his declaration.

"Does that mean...?"

She nodded. "I would be happy to call you husband."

He pressed a gentle kiss to her lips, placed the necklace around her neck, and held her close.

"Man of my heart," she whispered.

"I like the sound of that," he said.

"My mother calls my father that, even after all their years of marriage."

"It doesn't bother you we did this so soon?" he asked.

She shook her head but understood what he was saying. "My parents married soon after they met. According to mother, their love only grew stronger as time passed, and father says he loved her the first time he saw her."

He slumped in relief and kissed her again. She said yes!

"And who declares if it's too soon? The heart doesn't measure time; it measures love," she stated.

"Good, because I fell in love with you that first night we met," he offered.

She smirked. "Yes, you asked me if I liked cheese."

"I must have sounded like an imbecile of the highest order."

She shook her head. "No, it's a memory I'll cherish forever. My heart demands you, and I happily submit to the demand."

She nuzzled his goatee and ran her fingertips over his mustache. "This is something I'll have to get used to feeling. The men of my people don't have hair on their faces, but it's very becoming on you."

Wedding at Noon

S he let out a nervous breath before she entered The Old Rylanos Inn and patted her heated cheeks. She and Casden were going to tell a very protective elder about their engagement. It would be obvious anyway when he saw the betrothal necklace. She felt galvanized with Casden's hand on the small of her back, guiding her through the crowded dining room. The two arrived at Danarin's table, and all the talk stopped at their appearance.

"Good evening, plainsmen, and you as well, Master Dareld." she said.

Tyden saw the necklace, chuckled, and signaled a server for more wine. He was glad he accepted Danarin's supper invitation. It had been a while since things had been so lively.

"I see you used your mother's chain. She'd like that," Tyden said to Casden.

Doonay took a long look at the necklace and left the table. Aldren and Tholan followed to talk to him. It wasn't a matter for them, anyway. Danarin gestured for the couple to take a seat.

"When do you plan to wed?"

"Lidorn said that he would wed us tomorrow," she answered.

Danarin took her hand. "Are you sure, Naria? Once this is done, it can't be undone," he advised gently.

"I'm as sure of this as I am of being a druid. This man is of my heart," she said in the way of her people.

"And she is of mine," added Casden.

"Then I would say something good has finally come of this journey," Danarin stated and opened his arms, taking her into his embrace.

"Congratulations, young woman," he said, knowing that he had never felt more like a father than at that moment.

***

That night, Jezzine gathered a dozen other women from the Commons, and they threw an impromptu bridal party for Naria in the communal hall. Men were off-limits as food, drinks, and merry chatter echoed around the hall long into the evening. Eventually, the chat turned to naughty advice and jokes about wifely duties that caused Naria to choke on her drink and blush heavily. She wondered if half the talk she heard was the truth or something they said for fun.

The following day, Jezzine was beside herself with glee. "I've never stood with a bride before! You're going to be such a pretty one, too!" she gushed and carefully placed a wreath of delicate, tiny flowers on Naria's head.

The entire Temple Commons buzzed with the news, and word even made its way to the Royal Court. The Prince, Breddock, and his general were looking at a map of the southern continent and discussing water stores for the coming campaign.

"Breddock, what's happening in the magical quarter today? It's the place to be from what I hear," he quipped.

"A wedding at noon, from what I hear. The young Druid woman and a soldier."

"What's on my agenda today, old friend?" the prince asked.

"Aside from planning a campaign halfway across the continent, nothing, sire."

***

At midday, the plainsmen, the Temple Commons residents, a dozen of Casden's friends, and the remaining members of the Dareld family (minus Casden's brothers) gathered at the grove to wait for the betrothed couple. There was a commotion at the Temple Commons passageway when two Royal Guards marched through the entrance, followed by the Prince with the Regent at his side. The crowd bowed and curtsied upon his arrival at the grove.

"Fine day for a wedding," he noted.

A wizard at the temple shot fireworks from his wand when the betrothed couple appeared and started for the grove. The crowd parted to make a path for them, and the two stopped to stand before Lidorn. Naria clasped her hands in front of her and nodded.

"Honored brother, thank you for this gift," she said to Lidorn.

He nodded solemnly in return and began the ceremony. "Esteemed family, friends, and guests, today you will bear witness as Naria, daughter of Nidale; and Casden Dareld, son of Tyden Dareld, make their vows to join as husband and wife."

He spoke to Casden. "Casden, face the woman at your side. Is she the one of your heart?"

Casden faced her, and a loving smile graced his face. "Yes, she is the one of my heart."

"Naria, face the man at your side. Is this the man of your heart?"

"Yes, he is the man of my heart."

Jezzine and several women wiped their eyes with handkerchiefs. Aldren even gave his face a quick swipe. The love that emanated from the couple was palpable, a living force everyone could feel.

"Casden, make your pledge."

He cleared his throat and spoke. "Naria, today I ask to be your husband. I pledge to love only you until the breath of life leaves my body. I will love you in times of plenty or want, and when times are joyful or sad. Will you accept me as your husband?"

"I accept you with all of my heart," she replied.

He held up a ring adorned with a Naria stone his father had been holding. "See this circle that has no beginning and no end. It symbolizes my never-ending love," he recited and slid the ring on her finger.

"Naria, make your pledge."

She spoke, her gentle voice clear and strong. "Casden, today I ask to be your wife. I pledge to love only you until the breath of life leaves my body. I will love you in times of plenty or want, and when times are joyful or sad. Will you accept me as your wife?"

"I accept you with all of my heart," he returned.

She took a simple quilium band from Jezzine's outstretched palm. "See this circle that has no beginning and no end. It symbolizes my never-ending love," she recited and slid the ring on his finger.

Lidorn rested his hands on their shoulders and spoke. "Naria and Casden have pledged to join as husband and wife. They will kneel before one another to seal their pledges with the first kiss as husband and wife."

They kneeled and grasped their hands.

"Casden, by all means, kiss your pretty bride."

The crowd cheered and clapped as they kissed, fireworks shot in the air, and flower petals rained on the couple.

"Party in the dining hall!" Jezzine shouted.

***

The wedding celebration lasted for hours. Feasting, music, dancing, and merriment were the order of the day. The newlyweds sat at a place of honor at the head table, where they fed each other food and sweets from the feast. During their last dance at the party, he held her close.

"I only wish I could give you a wedding trip you deserve," he sighed, wanting her to have as much happiness as possible to sustain her for the days ahead.

"As long as we're together, it doesn't matter," she replied.

"You're easy to love, do you know that? Are all the women of your village as loving as you?"

"It's our wedding day, and you're already asking about other women?" she teased.

"How much wine have you had?" he asked.

"Just one small glass! It's not like beer, and I still feel like myself, just more relaxed," she said and lightly kissed his lips.

When they decided it was time to leave the celebration, she threw the wreath from her hair into the crowd. Jezzine caught it, which prompted Doonay and Tholan to tease Aldren in good fun. They left hand in hand, hearing the claps and cheers of the party guests following them until they left Temple Commons.

***

Tyden offered his home to the newlyweds for their short honeymoon. When they settled on the parlor couch, relieved to be away from the raucous crowd, she explained what would happen if they were in South Peak.

"There, the wedding celebration goes on long into the night. When the moon is at the highest point in the night sky, we would bathe each other in the river as a symbol of washing away our old life. Then we would go to our new home to... you know... and present ourselves to the Chief Elder at dawn."

"Hmm... we don't have a river nearby, but there is the bath basin. I like that tradition of yours. Are you nervous?"

She shrugged. "A little, but I know I shouldn't be because I'm with you."

"I'll make this night good for you, I promise."

During a bath filled with delightful discovery, she overcame her initial shyness, and they barely made it to his bedroom. She abandoned herself to the moment and surprised him with the power of her passion.

*****

She woke to the feel of a warm body pressed against her back, then feather-light kisses on her shoulders and neck. His arms wrapped around her, and she sighed, content.

"I won't mind waking from now on if I get to wake to this," she murmured, her voice husky.

He turned her over and kissed her. "It's almost dawn."

She nodded and ran her fingers lightly over his chest, tracing imaginary patterns, placing feather-light kisses here and there.

"Tease," he murmured, nipping an earlobe.

"Me?" she asked in mocking innocence.

"We have a couple of hours. How should we spend them?" he asked.

After a morning of loving, he made a pot of tea while she poked around the cupboards in the kitchen. "Do you and your father even eat? I'm going to be as hungry as a bear by lunchtime."

Casden heard knocking from the front door, and he answered it, greeting Danarin. They were to meet with the Regent and High General to review the South Peak campaign plans. She came from the kitchen with a cup of tea and smiled brightly at Danarin.

"Good morning!" she said brightly.

"To you as well, newlywed. We have a busy day ahead."

She drained her cup of tea and hugged her husband. "Take care today, husband."

"I would say the same to you, wife," he said.

Danarin quickly exited the home while they shared a heated kiss. A few minutes later, she left the home and secured her shawl to her shoulders.

***

Glancing around the street, she hoped that some food vendors were open early, but no such luck. *I'm starving, so of course not.* Her companions already waited on the front steps of Regent's Hall. She saw Aldren with two elppas, biting into a third.

"Aldren, dear Aldren, I'll give you a sky jewel for an elppa," she coaxed.

"Too busy for breakfast, newlywed?" he asked lightly, rolling the fruit around his palm.

So that's how it's going to be. She sighed and held out a hand. "Yes, happily busy."

Doonay rolled his eyes. Aldren contemplated her for a moment, grinned, and tossed her an elppa. Half of it was gone seconds after it landed in her hand. The doors opened, and a squire led them to a room with the Prince, the High General, and two cohort high sergeants. The Prince opened the meeting.

"Welcome, plainsmen. I know the campaign was to begin today, but my regent woke up with a fever this morning. I refuse to send him away ill."

He held up a hand at Naria's pending question. "Have no worries, a physician treated him. Come, let's examine the map."

A map of the southern continent covered the entire wall in an adjoining room. The High General stepped forward and spoke. "This campaign is straightforward, thank the heavens. It's a clear shot from here to South Peak," he said and made an imaginary line on the map with a wooden baton. "It'll be a six-day journey — providing the horses remain healthy and uninjured crossing the Golden Plains — on good ground, barring bad weather. We'll go with a cohort of five hundred infantry soldiers, a cohort of three hundred archers, and a company of scouts. What I need from you is a detailed map of South Peak and the surrounding lands."

He gestured to a large piece of blank parchment on a nearby table. "We'll stop a quarter-league from your village and send the scouts ahead. They'll assess the enemy's defenses and the position of your people. We'll surround the village with our forces and mount an advance just before sunrise to catch them unaware. The Regent will then make the ultimatum."

"What's the ultimatum?" asked Danarin.

The prince spoke. "Unconditional surrender. As a gesture of good sense, we'll request that they turn over the children first. We can't mount an advance with children underfoot. How many do you estimate are there?"

"Around fifty, your majesty," Naria answered.

"Have you had breakfast? We can work on the map after," the prince offered, and Naria shot Aldren a smug smile.

The rest of the morning, the companions worked with the High General on the South Peak map. Before they left, the Prince gave Naria a wedding gift. It was a painting of Rylanos with a view from the south, featuring the river west of the city and hills to the east.

"Thank you, your majesty. I'll always have a reminder of my time in this wondrous city."

"Before we leave, allow me to say that we are grateful for your help. South Peak will always be at your service, sire," stated Danarin.

***

That night, Naria picked up food for supper, and upon Jezzine's advice, scented bath oils. As she sliced bread, the front door opened.

"Anyone home?" Casden called.

"In the kitchen," he heard.

He entered, inhaled the food's aroma, embraced her from behind, and tickled her neck with light kisses. She shuddered with pleasure at her new favorite place for kisses.

"Delicious... the food too," he murmured.

Going North

The newlyweds made time for love and food the following day. He was pleased that her boldness and curiosity in the bedroom grew as she became more confident in herself. He was more than happy to let her play and explore. When they finally ate, she wrapped a sheet around herself, went to the kitchen, and brought a food tray back to bed.

"It's going to be a while before we get this again," she sighed.

"Most women would complain their heads off about living in the countryside," he noted.

"Not me. I'll feel so much better when I'm out there. I love all of it: clean air, the lush grasses, and the fresh water from the rivers. Beds and houses are nice, but druids are at their best among nature."

After breakfast, the plainsmen packed their belongings and left the inn. While Tholan and Doonay fetched the horses, Aldren and Danarin observed a growing argument among some Temple Commons residents. They quarreled over joining the South Peak campaign with brandished wands, even though none were asked to join the campaign.

"Just when I think I've heard it all, fighting to go to a fight. Look, that one was just poked in the eye with a wand," Aldren observed.

"It's been years since I've seen this much excitement in the Commons," Marden noted.

In Lidorn's mind, there was no doubt he was going. While unofficially Naria's mentor, he also felt a fatherly connection to her. He simply couldn't bear the thought of not being with her, especially if there was a battle, and he also looked forward to meeting her father. Marden understood and reluctantly agreed to stay behind. Rylanos needed a Druid. As for the mages…

"Naria, who else is going to watch your back?" Jezzine asked.

She decided she was going no matter what anyone said, even if she was booted from The Mage Guild. Naria was the kindest, most genuine friend she ever had, like the sister she never had. Naria's love, once given, was unconditional and tireless. There were two other reasons to go on the campaign she kept to herself: adventure and Aldren. She had lived her entire life in Port Hamaros or Rylanos. Outside of the two cities, she had seen nothing worth remembering for future storytelling. She knew she was capable of more than parlor tricks and wanted the opportunity to see and feel her true, deep magic in action. Magic that would terrify and enchant her opponents. Her master would be so proud!

As for Aldren, she knew he was a masterful hunter. No one could match his skill at tracking, and the only one to rival his strength was Doonay. If you didn't know him when you first met him, you would think of him as a fearsome fighter because of his size, strength, and skills. His people had no warriors, so it made sense that he didn't have a warrior mentality. She fell in love with her gentle giant's kind, humorous, affectionate nature. That nature would get him killed, and she would stop anyone who would try to take such a beautiful life from the world. She had to do everything she could to prevent that from happening. If he were to fall, she wouldn't be able to bear it.

Bristan was the first choice of The Wizard's Council. He was clumsy and absent-minded, but his combined power, fearlessness, and energy would make him a formidable opponent on the field of battle. Castanya disagreed and declared she would go instead, and Bristan objected in return. The arguments raged on, prompting Lidorn and the others to take their leave.

"They'll catch up," Lidorn quipped.

***

Outside of the city, the plainsmen readied their horses for the journey. Night whinnied in joy, literally chomping at the bit to stretch her legs on the prairie. Where was Garil? She didn't worry too much because he always appeared the time called for it.

"Where will your husband be?" Lidorn asked.

"He's among a company in the archer cohort. He says to look for a blue flag with seven arrows."

She would find him among the troops and travel with that part of the formation. He endured teasing from his fellows because he was the only married soldier on the campaign whose wife accompanied the troops. His company sergeant agree he could join his wife when they stopped for meals and rest, but be with his company when they moved. No one begrudged him for it.

To save time and avoid crowding, the archer cohorts left through the west gate, the infantry through the east gate. When the army left the city, the support caravan would follow. The weapon smith, armor smith, physician and medics, the Regent, and the High General had large oxen-driven covered wagons. Wagons for the cooks finished the caravan.

Naria gamboled Night outside the gates of the West Wall while company after company of archers rode out. Finally, a company that carried a blue flag with seven arrows rode from the gate. When Casden's company rode past the gate, he saw a beautiful black filly whinny loudly and shake out her mane. On the filly was his wife, her long brown hair blowing in the breeze. They made a pretty picture as the filly stamped the ground and strained against the bit in her excitement to stretch her legs in the open plains. Casden realized Naria didn't belong in the teeming, smelly city. Danarin should have been recognized for beautifying the city for bringing her there.

He rolled his eyes at the various comments from the soldiers. One would think they'd never seen a beautiful woman before.

"By the spirits, that's a sight worth fightin' for."

"There's a whole village of them women?"

"She's good on a horse."

"Dareld, you sod, how'd you get that lucky?"

Casden took one last look back at the city. He saw his father atop the West Wall raise a hand. Casden raised his hand in return. *Goodbye, father. I'll bring your grandchildren back to meet you.*

***

The army had traveled eight leagues by the end of the day, and the High General was pleased with the pace. A stone's throw from the Seventh Archers, Naria unsaddled Night, brushed her down, and set a generous picket for her to roam. After, set up her tent and started a fire. The soldiers posted watches for the night and lined up for supper behind the cook's wagon.

"See you in the morning," Casden quipped to his squad and left to join his wife for the night.

"Lucky sod," his squad members grouched good-naturedly at his back.

"I am a lucky sod," he agreed, sat down beside her, and held her close.

She relaxed in his embrace and resumed her discussion with Doonay. "... I know we're used to going faster, but there are eight hundred soldiers here after all, and they bear all their armor and equipment," she said and waved at her companions as they approached. "How was your ride today? Have a seat, and we can talk while supper cooks."

Jezzine and Bristan made an unexpected appearance out of thin air, startling Tholan, Doonay, and Danarin, not yet accustomed to their magic. Naria and Aldren grinned at each other. They were used to the magic.

"Welcome! Supper's cooking," Naria said.

"Where have you been?" Aldren asked, his feelings torn at seeing Jezzine there.

Jezzine wasn't in the Army and didn't have to go. Of course, he was glad to see her, but they were on their way to a battle after all.

"After we left Rylanos, we realized we forgot something, so we went back for it. Then we traveled back to the cook's wagon," Jezzine explained. "The cook also mentioned that a squirrel made the trip but was well behaved and ate nothing."

"How did you travel to the wagon? Ran and caught up with it?" Aldren asked.

"Magic," Jezzine casually stated and took a piece of bread Naria offered.

"Why did you stay in the wagon all day?" Doonay asked.

"I had no intention of walking across the hot plains all day," Jezzine returned.

"I'll let you ride my horse," offered Aldren.

"I don't know how to ride a horse," replied Jezzine.

"How can that be?" Doonay asked.

"I'll be happy to show you how it's done," Aldren answered, trying to draw attention away from another one of Doonay's short-sighted remarks.

Jezzine took it for what it was worth. She heard all about Doonay from Naria. How could she even have considered, for a single minute, to be with that oaf? *When he opens his mouth, the good looks vanish like magic.*

"How did you convince Castanya to stay behind?" Jezzine asked.

Bristan massaged his temples and looked at the sky with a sigh. "She didn't have a choice."

"Bristan, what did you do?" Jezzine accused.

"I spelled her into a night cat again. No one can undo the enchantment this time but me," he admitted.

"What if you die? She'll be a big black cat forever?" Aldren asked.

"No, if I die, the enchantment dies with me. She probably hates me now, but it's better for her to be alive and hating me than dead."

"What does the prince think of you joining the campaign?" Danarin asked.

"No disrespect intended to his majesty, but what he thinks doesn't matter," Jezzine stated.

Bristan nodded in agreement. "We are magi. We go when and where we please."

"Our skills will be useful. Just think of Bristan as a magical warrior," Jezzine said confidently.

I'll have to think hard about that, Naria thought and glanced pointedly at Lidorn.

"What about you?" Aldren asked of Jezzine.

"Hmm... with my magic, I've decided to annoy my enemies, terrify them, then annoy them some more," she said.

There was a collective shudder among the group at her casual declaration.

"We're Druid, we protect," Naria said of herself and Lidorn.

***

When the stew was finished, everyone produced bowls except for Jezzine and Bristan. Even the soldiers removed bowls from their packs before they filed behind the food wagon.

"Lesson learned, always carry a bowl," Bristan noted.

"No matter," Jezzine said, found two rocks, and transformed them to bowls.

"Thank you for allowing us to eat with you; the line at the food wagon is quite long," said Bristan.

"You'll always be welcome at my fire," Naria replied.

"You can't just make food appear?" Doonay asked.

"Now, that's a good question. There are some things you can't just conjure out of thin air. Mainly food, love, and money," Jezzine explained.

Casden reclined against Night's saddle, enjoying the good food and pleasant company after a hot, long day of riding. Being with his lovely new wife like this could almost make him forget the reason for the journey. He knew his part of the fight but was consumed with worry for Naria. She said she would protect, but at what cost? She was the most selfless person he had ever known, which meant she would put someone else's life above her own without hesitation. Just the thought of it felt as if his heart were squeezed. Naria sensed his unease and moved away from the fire to recline on the saddle with him.

"Something troubles you, my heart?" she asked.

How many times had she heard her mother ask her father that very thing?

"I remember you saying that sometimes your thoughts become too much. What do you do?"

"Talk with someone or commune with the spirits."

"Commune with the spirits?"

"Meditation and prayer. I can teach you if you'd like."

"I'd rather talk; not sure how good I'd be with that spirit talk."

"Let's settle in my... *our* tent so we can talk in private."

The two bid everyone a good night and retired to their tent. Once in his arms, she soothed his troubled mind with calming caresses and words of love, hope, and encouragement.

***

The following morning, after heaping bowls of breakfast porridge, Casden was sent back to his company with a kiss and honey cakes. Today was also the day that Jezzine and Bristan were to ride horses for the first time. Aldren would have Jezzine on nothing other than his horse, while Bristan felt more comfortable with Naria and Night.

"Listen, the lady's never rode a horse, so be good," Aldren told his horse.

The horse flicked his tail and waited patiently while Aldren ensured Jezzine was seated correctly in the saddle.

"What if he gets tired?" Jezzine asked.

The horse turned around and whinnied at her as if to say *you wish!*

"Well, pardon me, horsey," Jezzine declared.

Aldren laughed. "I don't ride him all day long; I walk sometimes. Doonay is the biggest among us, and if a horse can handle him, you should be no problem."

"Does this horse have a name?" she asked.

Aldren nodded. "His name is Brillon."

When the army stopped for food and rest at midday, Casden joined the plainsmen and saw that Naria wasn't with them.

"Where's my wife?"

Danarin pointed behind the army toward the open plains. "She's back there a-ways. The wizard's never ridden a horse. They'll catch up."

Not long later, Night ambled to them with Bristan astride her, smiling brightly. "That was fantastic; I don't know why I've never ridden before. Thank you, Night," he said, patting Night's neck.

He slid off the saddle and led Night to the plainsmen's horses.

"I'll fetch Naria," he said and disappeared in front of their eyes.

A minute later, he reappeared with Naria. She looked around with wide, astonished eyes.

"It would have taken me an hour to catch up!" she exclaimed.

Bristan and Jezzine smiled at Naria's wonder. Naria could call down the rain and make the ground tremble, but she was amazed at a trick a ten-year-old mage could perform.

"Have you been walking since after breakfast?" Casden asked.

Naria nodded and tore into a piece of bread.

"You must be parched," he scolded said and gave her a water skin.

"Don't look worried. We're people of the plains, so walking on the plains isn't a chore. However, I look forward to a bath."

Jezzine wished she felt more at home on the plains, and she wished it even more when it rained that night. Casden shared Naria's tent, so he let Jezzine use his army-issued tent for shelter. She wasn't accustomed to life on the trail, and he felt a bit sorry for her, but she didn't complain. With a spell, she enlarged the tent so that Bristan and the plainsmen could also sleep under shelter. *It's the least I can do for them to put up with me. They must think I'm ridiculous.* Aldren didn't believe she was ridiculous and asked if he could place his bedroll closer to hers. In the corner, they murmured into the night.

∗∗∗

On the third day of the journey, old language lessons continued. Naria would say a word, and then Bristan would say it in Wizard tongue.

"Hold on, one or the other! My mind can only do so much!" Aldren interjected.

"Since the old language is still used all over the continent, but only wizards know wizard tongue, we should stick with the old language," Tholan pointed out.

Inside his wagon, the prince overheard the companion's banter throughout the day and thought it priceless. He agreed with Tholan because he didn't know the old language, so he was learning. The companions agreed with Tholan, so Naria continued.

"Let's continue with the world. Sial, sky. So'sial, cloud. Tho'sial, rain."

"F'sana felia."

"I've heard that before," Jezzine said.

"Yes, my nickname, falling leaf. F'sana, falling. Felia, leaf."

That night, Doonay and Aldren gained additions to their wagering game of sticks and rocks in the dirt when soldiers got wind of it. Tholan was happy to be of use, repairing the rickety wheels of the weapon smith's wagon and mending a broken seat that almost sent the cook tumbling off his wagon. Danarin was deep in conversation at the Regent's wagon while Jezzine and Bristan entertained a large group of soldiers with various feats of magic. Naria and Casden were sitting away from the camp at their own fire. As they gazed at the stars, she told a tale of why there were so many stars in the night sky.

"The first bear, the father of all bears today, climbed a mountain to see where all the bears were in the world. As he neared the top of the highest peak, he became covered with snow. Fearing that he would become weighed down with too much snow and die on the mountain, he prayed for the strength to shake the snow from his fur. As night fell, the spirits granted his wish, and he shook the snow from his coat, throwing the snow in all directions high into the sky. Not wanting to waste their creation, the spirits kept it in the sky with them."

"Did your father tell you that story?" he asked.

"No, my mother. Our people spend many nights around fires telling tales. Father told me mostly druid legends."

"My mother told stories, but I was young and can scarcely remember them. When she died, the stories died with her. Tell me another?" he requested.

She gave him a quick hug and pointed to the east. "Do you see that pattern of stars on the east horizon?" she asked.

"The one that looks like a horse?"

She nodded. "When the moon is again full in the sky, the pattern will be different, a rider to go with the horse."

"I'll take care to notice it. Just how many stories do you know?" he asked.

She tapped her temple. "A lifetime's worth. Enough to keep our children entertained for many nights around a fire."

***

In the late afternoon, the army arrived at the river that marked the halfway point in the journey. The General called for the army to halt for the day, and soldiers were assigned to replenish the water stores. The fresh, cool water did wonders for the weary bodies of everyone making the ride across the arid plains.

"We bathe tonight," Jezzine said.

Naria heartily agreed. "Indeed."

In her tent that evening, Naria mended a tunic and chatted with Jezzine while the soldiers bathed. They stripped down to their underpants and poured buckets of water over their bodies or submerged themselves in the river. She had no desire to watch, and Jezzine pretended not to. However, she cast surreptitious glances from behind the tent flap, hoping to catch a glimpse of Aldren as he bathed. Casden joined them in the tent, which prompted Jezzine to leave in case they got romantic.

"I thought to wait later for a bath," he hinted.

"Hmm, I thought the same," she replied.

"There's a pleasant spot down the river a bit, away from prying eyes," he suggested.

"Perhaps you can show me this pleasant spot," she said, leaning in for a kiss.

"You keep that up and I'll forget how grimy I am," he said.

She put her face to his neck and inhaled. "You smell of the plains. I like that smell."

He felt her lips softly touch his neck. "You taste..." she said and gave his neck a nip, "salty."

He fastened the tent flap, and bathing was forgotten for the time being.

***

On the fourth day of the journey, the group told their favorite memories of their childhood. Bristan spoke first. "Mine is of the day I first met my master, the day I turned ten years old. He asked me to show him what I knew and handed me his wand. I blew up his bed accidentally, of course. Even with magic, cleaning up the feathery mess took a long time."

Doonay was next. "The day I came of age, my sixteenth birthday. I hunted on my own that day for the first time and brought home a bear. It was a lot of meat, and my father was glad to have a new blanket from the skin."

He glanced at Naria, and she realized that she still had his prized bear tooth necklace. Just one more awkward moment in her life, she supposed.

"Oh, I have one!" Jezzine called out, startling Aldren's horse. "The first anniversary of being with my master, my parents came to visit when I turned eleven. They clapped at the bouquet I conjured for my mother. They clapped and cheered; that's my favorite memory."

"The day I helped my mother birth to my littlest sister," Tholan said.

"I remember Father arrived just after," Naria said.

"The day my daughter was born, that was a fine day," Danarin said and urged his horse ahead of the others.

"Why does he leave?" Bristan asked.

"It's a wonderful memory, but a sad one as well. His daughter died two years ago," Naria explained.

"What of his wife? He'll be happy to see her again after all this renegade business is said and done," said Jezzine.

"She died as well," answered Doonay.

"How sad," Bristan stated.

"But he bears it well," remarked Jezzine.

"Which is why he's an elder. Aside from our chief elder, he's the wisest and most even-tempered of the bunch," Tholan explained.

"Aldren? Naria? We haven't heard from you yet," Jezzine said.

Aldren tapped his chin. "Hmm... so many memories to choose from."

"I'll bet," Naria murmured.

"Well, it would have to be the day of my first hunt as well. I was so impressed with Doonay's hunt that I hunted bear too. I dressed in antlers and deer skins and crept around the woods for hours until I finally found one. I chased the bear, he chased me, and at some point we both found ourselves stuck in mud bogs, ten paces from each other. Neither one of us could get out. We stared at each other for hours; I talked to the bear as he huffed and growled at me."

"Your turn, F'sana Felia," Jezzine urged.

Naria nodded. "By the time I was eight, I could make salves. They were often wrong, and my father liked to tease me about it. One morning, as I made a salve, my friends called me out to play. So out I went and forgot about my bowl of salve on the table. When my father returned home and saw the bowl, he thought it was porridge, so he sat down and took a big bite. How horrid it must have tasted! But it was funny that my mother watched it all happen and didn't say a word. She figured it was in return for all the teasing, so that's why my father says that fate isn't as fickle as we think."

Soldiers and Scoundrels

On the morning of the sixth day, there was an air of restlessness among the soldiers expecting action. Among the companions, the silence of uncertainty made every clip of their horse's hooves seem louder. Aldren looked to Doonay, then Doonay to Tholan, and all looked askance at Naria. She was lost in her musings astride Night. Would they, and could they, fight? How would they feel to see their people under the menace of renegades? None of them had ever raised a spear or arrow to someone in anger. *Except for me, who charged at a man as a drooling, snarling wolf!*

While Naria worked to carve a new pattern on her staff after supper, Aldren voiced his concerns about the possibility of violence.

"It's hard for me to imagine harming another, but what if it's to save a life? I don't think I can just stand by while someone is hurting others," he conceded.

"Just how peaceful are we when faced with something like this?" Tholan wondered.

"Knowing when to fight and not to fight? No one can know that until the moment is upon them," Lidorn said.

"These are hard questions," Danarin stated.

They all looked to Naria when she dropped a knife and her staff, and an angry, muted *"lankash, again!"* fell from her lips. Casden took her hand to examine the cut.

"I don't believe my ears. Naria said a bad word," Aldren teased.

"We need to settle our thoughts before getting there," Naria said, shaking her thumb and sucking on the blood. "I've tried the entire journey, and there are some things I realize."

"Tell us, young druid," a voice said.

Casden jumped to his feet at the sight of the High General behind the group of companions. He waved Casden back down.

"Stay with your wife, corporal. I've been curious about this separate camp you all keep. As you were saying?"

"We have a surprise on our side. We have seen no renegades yet, so they don't know that we approach with an army of proper soldiers. They've done wrong, and we are going to right that wrong. Knowing that, how can we lose? In my mind, we've already won the important part of all this," she said.

"I don't understand," Doonay said.

"Plainsman, the young woman describes the battle of the mind. When an army is superior in that aspect, no one can defeat it. Weak focus leads to weak action. Strong focus leads to strong action."

"I understand that," Doonay said.

"At our village, the people are held captive by renegades thinking of riches, not us," Danarin pointed out.

"We're prepared to fight, and they're not. The simplicity of it is something I don't see often. It should work to our advantage," the High General said.

Naria rested her head on Casden's shoulder and yawned.

"I see that some of us are ready to sleep," the General said. "Enjoy your wife's company, and I bid good night to the rest of you."

"General, take some," Naria said and held some honey cakes out for him.

***

Late that afternoon, the General announced for the army to stop and summoned the plainsmen.

"I recognize where we are. I passed through this country on my vision quest. South Peak is less than half a day away," Naria said, and her companions nodded in agreement.

"Excellent. I'll send scouts to determine our exact position. As planned, we'll move to a quarter-league from the village."

While the scouts prepared to travel light, Naria was so anxious that she voiced an idea to shift to her wolf form and see the village for herself. The plainsmen immediately balked at the idea, which exasperated her. She might not be as big and strong as they were, but she was just as brave.

"I'll just see what the General thinks," she finished primly and marched away.

"Doonay, find Casden. He might talk some sense into her," urged Danarin.

The general pondered her idea as he paced in front of his wagon and spoke with the with the scout captain. "One of you with the scouts as they survey the village... as a wolf.... tactically, it's a good idea. You know this area best. Too bad the rest of the scouting party can't go as wolves."

"I would go with you, but a wolf *and* bear loping together would attract unwanted attention," Lidorn said.

"The sight of a bear alone would attract attention. There's no bear this far west," Aldren said.

Danarin threw up his hands. Why were they even considering this? Naria was no scout!

"If we wait until night, even better," the General said and nodded. "It's settled. The Druid in her wolf form will join the scout company tonight to see the enemy's position and defenses."

Doonay returned. "The soldiers are at a weapons drill, but Casden said to expect him at supper. He wasn't happy."

***

Casden wanted to shake Naria to her senses at supper when she told him about the plans. "You're not a soldier! Why must you do this? It's too dangerous!" he pleaded, trying to make her see reason.

"My heart, if it were your home, wouldn't you do everything you could to help? I'll be a wolf in the dark, in the tall grass; they won't even know I'm there. If they see me, all they'll see is a wolf. No one knows the land better than one of us. I'll be with the scouts, and if things go wrong, I can run faster than any of them," she reasoned.

"Naria, this is no joking matter," Casden chastised.

"I'm not joking; Lidorn says I'm fast for a wolf," she said. "Please believe in me. I can do this. I'm not afraid."

"You should be," he retorted.

The Seventh Archer's company high sergeant shouted, "Dareld! Front and center!"

Casden reported to him and stood at attention before him. "Stand easy, corporal. The captain has allowed you to join the scouts on tonight's mission."

He leaned closer and spoke in an undertone. "They can use an extra bow, and aside from that, it's too much to ask of you to just watch your wife trot off to danger. Go quickly; take only your bow."

He winked at Casden and nodded at the scout company. "There'll be other wolves as well."

***

Nidale walked among his people along the riverbank, bringing them what comfort he could. *If only someone could do the same for me.*

When druids could not fulfill their calling, their powers faltered, and Nidale knew it was happening to him. He tried not to give in to despair, but the soul-deep sadness was becoming too much to bear. No one could take belongings from the village on their forced departure, not even his healing kit. Lanard was highly suspicious of him and wouldn't allow anything that could be used against him. He let the people take only food so that his soldiers didn't have to waste time and resources to feed them. Worst of all was the loss of his staff. The essence of his power was the staff he'd had since he was a boy, so faltering power and no staff equaled a weak and incapable druid. Were it not for his wife, he would have already gone mad. Not so long before, he had been a strong druid of a noble, independent people. Now they labored relentlessly, digging in the dirt for gems, and his heart broke more for them with each passing day. Some were forced to rebuild lodging for the renegades, but most shoveled and sifted through the soil from sunrise to sunset. He made to return to his wife when he heard a commotion from the guards at the bridge.

"That wolf's only twenty paces away! My blind mother can hit it!" one bragged.

"What mother?!" another challenged.

Nidale looked beyond the bridge and saw a wolf trotting about an area just beyond the bridge. A pack of wolves came into sight, meandering about the area. The wolf at the bridge saw him, stopped, and howled mournfully at the moon.

"Quiet, mangy beast!" one guard complained, and another guard from the bridge shot an arrow at it. It landed a pace from the wolf's snout, which caused it to yap in alarm and run away faster than any wolf he had ever seen.

***

Hours later, when the scouting party returned and reported to the General, Naria returned to herself and cried sorrowfully. Casden held her as she cried and beat on his chest as he shook in his boots. During the scouting mission, he'd been lying in the tall grasses with an arrow ready to fly. In his opinion, she had wandered entirely too close to the renegade-laden bridge. He kept an anxious watch on her and ten of the scouts who sportingly agreed to go as wolves as well, thanks to Bristan. Seeing an arrow land footsteps from her snout left him shaking in his boots back to camp.

While concerned arrows had flown, Bristan had been thrilled. Someone wanted him to make a transformation, and ten of them at that! Even better, he could reverse the change. In his mind's eye, he could see Jezzine watch him skeptically as he performed the incantations. Would he ever live down spelling his woman into a night cat?

"What has happened?" Danarin asked upon seeing Naria so upset.

"I saw Father! He was right there in the village, looking out over the river. All I could do was howl!"

"One of those scoundrels shot an arrow at her!" fumed Casden, shuddering again at the memory.

"Blast! I knew I should have joined you!" Jezzine exclaimed.

"So someone can shoot at you, too?" Aldren asked.

Danarin held his hands up. "All right, everyone, let's just calm down. No one was hurt."

Casden knew the both of them needed calming, but what could he do?

"Do you want a bath?" he asked Naria.

She sniffed and looked at him like he'd had too much beer. "A bath? Now?"

"I know you feel dirty after being a wolf. It might help you feel better."

After everyone had settled down for the night, the couple lovingly washed the day's grime from each other's weary bodies. He might die tomorrow, so it might be the last night he would feel his loving wife in his arms. He was going to cherish every second.

***

As the sun rose, Naria made a pot of porridge for whoever wanted some. Neither she nor her companions had an appetite until Casden finally coaxed her into eating at least a piece of bread. They went to the Regent's wagon to meet with the General, and Casden joined his company.

"This is a momentous day for you, I'm sure. Thanks to the scouts, we know where to approach. We'll break off into four formations and surround the village from all four directions. I'll approach the bridge when the army is in place to make the ultimatum."

The regent addressed the druids. "I know this is asking much, but do you mind joining me in your animal forms? It'll send a message to our enemy that we have magic users should you decide to return to yourselves in front of them. I've always believed in the might of swords over magic, but in this case, it's an element of surprise that I can't pass up."

Jezzine and Bristan glanced at each other pointedly. They had a plan as well.

"I, for one, would like to see the look on their faces when they see the Regent approach with a bear and a wolf," Lidorn said.

"I insist on being there as well," Danarin stated.

"That's a sound idea. We'll be close enough to the village for your people to see, and they'll be inspired by the sight of you confronting this man."

Casden was with his company, readying to approach the village from the north. He saw the Regent in full armor giving instructions to the High General.

"General Merdant, if I fall, you will take charge of this campaign. Carry out his majesty's orders."

Danarin, Naria, Lidorn, and a soldier joined the Regent, and they started toward the bridge. Naria broke from the group and hurried towards

Casden. The company of soldiers parted to clear a path for her. She pushed his helm up enough to give him a heated kiss.

"Take care, husband. You'll meet my parents tonight, and I'll make you supper at my home. I love you with all that I am."

"What is this? What are you doing?" he asked, alarmed.

"Didn't you know? I'm getting my home back," she said with a wink, transformed into a wolf, and ran back to the Regent.

THE BATTLE

"Hurry with that food! Daylight's wasting!" Commander Lanard shouted.

He thought he felt the ground tremble ever so slightly, then some men shouted and pointed at the rise to the north where hundreds of horses appeared. From the west, archers on the horses dismounted and took their weapons in hand. More hooves echoed, and hundreds more horses emerged beside the wooded area east of the village. The infantry dismounted and placed their hands on their hilts, shields at the ready. To the south and west embankments, more infantry and archers appeared.

As a whole, the people of South Peak stood, their breakfast forgotten.

"Thank the heavens!" villagers cried out.

"What the devil is that supposed to be? A fancy man with his pets?" a renegade asked and pointed beyond the bridge.

The fully armored regent, a soldier, and Danarin approached the bridge. The unusual sight was the bear loping beside the Regent and a wolf in front.

"It's Danarin!" a villager shouted.

Nidale and the other elders rushed to the front of the villagers to get a good look at the approaching party. Danarin was carrying two staves, walking to the right of an armored man. They stopped, and the soldier hoisted a white flag in the air. Leeda joined her husband and took his hand.

"Why in the world would Danarin and that man be walking with those animals?" she asked.

"The animals are druids," Nidale stated.

The surrounding villagers gasped in amazement.

"Surely one of those animals isn't our Naria!" Leeda said. "Surely, she wouldn't risk herself by returning!"

"By returning with help to free us," Nidale concluded, his heart bursting with love and pride for his daughter.

"Look, there's my son!" Doonay's father shouted and pointed to the wooded area to the east.

Aldren's mother cried out, "Aldren is there too!"

Lanard realized he was losing control of the situation and turned to the man beside him. "I'll see what this animal-loving buffoon has to say. Do nothing until I return," he warned.

The man saluted with a fist to his chest and glanced nervously at the villagers behind him. The commander ran his hands through his hair and walked over the bridge.

The Regent stopped twenty paces before the bridge and rested his hand on the pommel of his sword. *Let this scoundrel come to me.* The soldier behind him unsheathed his sword at Lanard's approach.

Lanard stopped ten paces before the Regent, not knowing what to make of the animals. The growling wolf paced back and forth in front of the group. The bear huffed and rose on his back legs.

"Is Naria the wolf or bear?" Leeda wondered.

Lanard swallowed heavily and took a step back when the bear rose. The Regent removed his helm and placed it under his arm. He projected an image of dismissal of the man's presence, giving Lanard a scathing look from head to foot. When he spoke, his voice reflected his disgust. His eyes were rigid and unwavering.

"I am Breddock Nalmor, regent for the Prince of this realm. Your name is unimportant, cur, but what is important are my next words. Within the hour, you and this dubious army will put down your weapons, release these people, and submit yourselves to the mercy of the prince's justice. There will be no conditions, for your crimes are beyond negotiation. Failure on your part will cause drastic action on our part. As you can see, you are surrounded and outnumbered by superior forces."

He let his words settle to the flabbergasted renegade commander.

Bristan and Jezzine appeared behind a platoon of renegades in the village with a soft pop. Bristan flicked his wand, and the men were rooted in place, unable to move their feet. A second later, they found their lips closed, unable to open. Jezzine cleared her throat and spoke.

"Now that we have your attention, please note that you cannot move your feet or talk. You are also the only ones that can see or hear me, for the moment."

One of them grabbed his sword and snatched his hand away. He looked at the burn on his palm, then at Jezzine in horror.

"You also cannot take your swords unless you want to be burned," advised Bristan.

"Clever," she quipped.

"Thank you."

She flourished her wand in the men's direction. A dozen buckets appeared over their heads, prompting Bristan to speak.

"We highly suggest that you surrender and make your way to the nearest group of Rylan soldiers surrounding this village. If you surrender peacefully, no harm will come to you."

She waved her hand again, and the buckets upended, dumping mud on the men. "This is just a taste of what you'll face if you choose not to surrender. Swords and arrows will be the least of your problems," she warned.

They disappeared with a pop.

"They have magi," one man whined.

***

"As a show of reason on your part, I insist you release the children. Now."

"Now?" Lanard snarled.

"Yes, now. I do not mean tomorrow, cur."

Lanard turned on his heel, grumbling about being called a cur. He marched over the bridge and stood nose to chin with Nidale.

"You planned this, didn't you?" he demanded.

"I wish I had," Nidale returned.

"Insolence!" Lanard shouted and punched Nidale in the stomach.

On the other side of the river, the wolf snarled loudly, her ears erect and forward. Crouched, with bristled fur from ruff to tail, the wolf was angry, pawing the ground and ready to fight. Now Nidale was sure the wolf was his daughter. The bear huffed and nudged the wolf's flank.

"Strike that man again, and the wolf won't be held back!" the Regent called out.

"Release the children, he says. Call me cur, does he? I'll release them all right, as I see fit!" he grumbled.

"You and you!" he called out, pointing to two women. "Gather the girl children and set them loose. To the bridge, wenches!"

Naria heard the cries of girls too frightened to leave their families and she shifted back to woman form, sending fireballs high into the air to get their attention.

"This way, girls, hurry!" she called.

"Girls, run to Naria!" Leeda and many other women urged.

The girls ran to the bridge, and Lidorn returned to himself. His eyes glowed as he glared at the renegades on the opposite side of the bridge, causing half a dozen water cyclones to dance on the river's surface. The renegades hurried the girls as if speeding them along would lessen the magical wrath waiting for them. The first of the girls met Danarin, and he pointed to the company of scouts across the field.

"Girls, do you see the brown horse in front? Run to the men by the horse!" he urged, picked up a small girl, and led the way.

"Hurry, precious ones, go quickly," Breddock urged.

Some girls gave Naria hurried hugs when they passed by, and tears streamed down her face as they ran past her. As Danarin led the girls to the scout company, he looked back and decided that Naria would be safe with Lidorn.

Casden watched the tense scene from the rise, gripping his bow so hard that he thought he might break it in half. Why was his wife shooting fireballs into the air? He was agitated, watching her standing there a mere twenty paces from renegades with ready swords and bows. He saw the scouts were leading the girls to the safety of the support wagons a half-league away. Danarin, the older girls, and the scouts carried as many smaller ones as possible. Why wasn't Naria running with them?

"That's a brave wife you have there, Dareld," the man next to him commented.

After the girls were out of sight, Lanard sneered and spat in the Regent's direction.

"Fool," Breddock muttered.

"Call me cur, will you? You want the rest, come and get 'em!" Lanard challenged.

"One hour, cur!" the Regent called and turned on his heel.

His guard followed him back to the west cohort while Lidorn and Naria stayed near the bridge.

"Why is she still there?" Leeda asked.

"Did you think she was going to leave?" Nidale asked.

A man and woman suddenly appeared next to Leeda, trying to blend in with the crowd.

"They've brought magi as well," Nidale said.

"We're going to get as many of the remaining children out as we can," Bristan said.

"Don't be startled when you see them vanish," Jezzine advised.

"Perhaps we can provide a distraction," Lidorn offered, noting the subtle movement of the magi among the crowd.

"That would be helpful; many thanks," Bristan said.

Nidale looked to the elders. "We need to keep the people together as much as possible; we can't be scattered. Quietly pass the word along," he said and looked across the river.

He saw Naria twirl her staff, keenly feeling the loss of his staff more than ever. Bristan and Jezzine were in and out of the village in seconds with three to four children at a time. They appeared and disappeared so fast that the renegades didn't notice him. Nor did they notice the mage that cast a spell to disillusion groups of children and lead them to the wooded area to the east. The renegades were too distracted by Naria calling the wind.

"N'riss n'dar!"

Her eyes glowed, and she wielded her staff, chanting words known only to Druid. Blazing winds blew the water over the riverbank, dousing the nearby renegades, while another gust blew Lanard's lodge to pieces. Nidale proudly watched his daughter commune with the spirits of the wind.

***

As the hour was approaching an end, Breddock noted that no children were left in the village. The magic users did a splendid job, so the General signaled the soldiers to the east to move closer to the village. If the fight moved east, Doonay, Aldren, and a company of soldiers would stay with the boys who evacuated to the woods.

Naria stopped the winds and took stock of the situation. She was closest to the village, with the southern cohort behind her and the bridge in front of her. The soldiers to the east had moved closer, and the remaining Rylan cohorts were also closing in. It looked as if there was going to be a fight, and the thought tore at her heart. She looked across the field to Lidorn, pressed her hand to her heart, and nodded. He nodded in return and turned to talk to Breddock. She returned her attention to the village and bridge, again twirling her staff. Nidale saw Naria take in the situation, acknowledge the other druid, and twirl her staff. *Daughter, what will you do?*

Lanard finally noticed that the children were gone. He cursed and stomped around the remains of his lodge.

"Commander, maybe we should—" an underling suggested.

"Should we what? Just run away with our tails tucked between our legs because of a few tricks? And why are you riff-raff covered in mud?!" he demanded.

The men covered in mud thought that leaving was an excellent suggestion. They still couldn't touch their swords and were worried that the magi would appear and do something even more frightening to them.

"If a fight's what they want, then that's what they'll get! I don't care how many soldiers they have! Put arrows in the magi scum first chance you get! Better yet, run 'em through slowly with a blade!"

The General commanded the army to advance, further enraging Lanard. "Let 'em get close and attack when I give the command!" he bellowed.

Now a desperate man, he was losing face in front of the men and would lose the riches in the ground if he didn't fight for it.

"Shields at the ready!" the Rylan company commanders called.

Bristan and Jezzine grasped arms and wished each other good fortune. "As planned, I'll be with the soldiers," he said.

"I'm with the plainsmen," Jezzine stated.

Both disappeared with a pop. Jezzine reappeared in a tree to the east and waited while she kept an eye on Naria. Aldren and Doonay were below her with the soldiers ushering the children into the woods. She whistled softly, and they looked up. She waved, and they smiled.

"Magic!" one boy called out excitedly.

She put a finger to her lips and winked.

***

"Three-step advance, march!" the infantry commanders called. From the east and west positions, they marched three steps and paused, then three more.

"Bows at the ready!" the archer commanders called.

They had been given instructions not to shoot until shot upon and to take extra care not to hit the villagers. Meanwhile, the Druids were worsening the weather, spooking the renegades even more.

"N'riss n'hav!" Naria sang, south of the village.

"N'riss n'thon!" Lidorn called, west of the village.

Staves raised and eyes glowing, Lidorn called deafening thunder while Naria called the wind and rain. The raging thunderstorm stopped when the Rylan soldiers were within a hundred paces of the village. Lanard felt the world closing in on him.

"Arrows! Loose!" he screeched.

Jezzine furiously waved her hands, and the quivers of the nearby renegades fell from their waists and stuck to the ground. The Rylan soldiers in the woods advanced on the renegades tugging at their quivers, trying to pry them off the ground.

"Return fire!" the Rylan archer commanders shouted.

Dozens of renegades fell on the first barrage. Naria saw arrows heading toward her people, and her breath caught in her throat, but they came to stop mid-air and fell harmlessly around them. She let out a cry of relief when she saw Jezzine was among them. Relief fell to dismay when Doonay faltered and fell, holding his leg. She saw an arrow lodged in his thigh.

"No!" she shrieked, and earth-shaking thunder rumbled overhead.

Once again, her eyes glowed, and a cyclone left the river, traveling toward the nearest group of renegades. She raised her staff high in the air.

"N'riss iness!"

Nidale couldn't believe his eyes. Just how much power had his daughter discovered? He and a group of villagers took shelter under the bridge as they made their way toward the hopeful safety of the sacred grove.

From the west, the command was given for the infantry to attack. "Take the nearest renegades!"

Bristan appeared with the infantry and saw that the bridge was too narrow for the number to cross quickly. He charmed a portion of the river to become a hard surface for the soldiers to cross, another spell that enchanted a dozen renegades to sleep, and spelled another dozen to lose their sight. When he raised his arm for a flaming sword enchantment, he saw the flash of a sword. He felt agony and wonder when the sword slashed him from shoulder to stomach. *How could I have forgotten to cast a shield?* He fell to his knees, holding the still waters enchantment until all the soldiers were across the river. *I'll just rest here for a while.*

"I'm here, wizard," he heard and opened his eyes.

Lidorn kneeled next to him, applying healing herbs and bandages to the wound, ignoring the fighting over his shoulder.

"Naria's doing well," Bristan gasped.

"Indeed," Lidorn agreed, and glanced over his shoulder to see another hapless group of renegades caught up in the relentless wind and rain of the cyclones.

FE T'OBION

The villagers fled in groups to the sacred grove west and the wooded area east. Aldren was carrying an older woman in no condition to keep up with the fleeing crowd and lost sight of Doonay. When he got to the eastern woods, he saw the renegades were using whatever they could get their hands on as weapons. Jezzine was furiously casting shields to protect the villagers that were taking cover among the trees. She saw Aldren's face contort in pain, and he faltered, but he kept going with the older woman in his arms. He set the woman on her feet when he arrived at the tree line, and Jezzine saw an arrow lodged in his back.

"Aldren!" she screamed.

He didn't hear her and stepped in front of a renegade approaching a woman and her young son. He didn't see the flaming torch that struck his head and he fell to the ground. Jezzine, enraged, let terrifying magic consume her. The renegades found themselves swept into a flaming vortex, swirling about the northeast corner of the village. They were thrown from the vortex against trees, boulders, and fellow renegades as they burned. Lidorn was in bear form near the bridge between Bristan and the Rylan soldiers fighting the renegades. He knew he couldn't save the young wizard, but would stay with him to offer comfort until the end.

"Well done, Jezzine," Bristan whispered when he saw the flaming vortex. "Many thanks, druid."

His vision faded and he saw no more. Back in Rylanos, a woman who had been a night cat fell to her knees in sorrow.

When Nidale, his wife, and a group of villagers reached the grove, he urged them to take shelter in the den. *I don't think the spirits will mind this time.* More saw Nidale and were inspired to make their way to the relative safety of the grove as well. He ran back toward the battle despite his wife's pleas, urging him to return to the den. His daughter was fighting for their people, and he should do no less. He had been helpless for far too long.

Across the battlefield, Casden saw the wizard on the ground and feared for Naria more than ever. Twenty-six men from his company were wounded and could no longer fight, and he didn't know how many dead. He came close to joining the dead when an arrow ricocheted off his helm. *Too close!*

"Advance and keep on them!" was the command given.

There was fierce fighting at the bridge and south positions. Casden heard a horrible roar from the bear and saw him fall with two arrows in his neck. He rose again, and his enormous paw swiped clumsily at two nearby renegades. Casden shot an arrow into a man advancing on the bear. He and other archers grabbed abandoned swords from the ground and joined the infantry from the north positions. They moved on the renegade force to the south with triumphant battle cries.

The bear dropped to the ground with a final huff and fell still. The spirit of justice fled from Naria when she saw Lidorn fall. Vengeance came into its place. She raised her staff with both hands and called to the sky.

"N'riss n'bent!"

Lightning struck groups of renegades, causing their comrades to flee in terror. She brought her staff to the earth, and the land shook. Many of the remaining renegades dropped their weapons and begged for the quaking ground, thunderstorms, lightning strikes, and cyclones to stop. They ran away as fast as their feet could run when they saw her coming their way with fire in her hand.

Naria ran to the bridge to get to Lidorn and saw Bristan unmoving on the ground, his kind eyes open to the sky. Her eyes welled with sad, angry tears. She started across the bridge, taking no heed of the renegades begging for mercy as she passed. When she stepped from the bridge, she heard someone shout, "Look out!" and felt a painful impact on her right arm that spun her around. The fireball fell from her hand, and she found herself face to face with Lanard. His face only had one look, that of death. She had never been as frightened in her life as she was at that moment.

He slashed at her with his sword, and she blocked it with her staff, causing the blood from her injured arm to splatter them both. She blocked another slash but was knocked to the ground by its force. She rolled and jumped to her feet, feeling the heat on her back from the bridge that was now ablaze. Lanard tripped on Lidorn's abandoned staff and swore when an arrow embedded in his sword hand, causing the sword to slip from his hand. Undeterred, he pulled the arrow from his hand and snatched Lidorn's staff off the ground. He spat at her and resumed his attack.

She wasn't prepared for the jab to her side and ineffectively blocked it. The pain took her breath away, and he swung again. She stopped his swing again, but caught a glancing blow to the head that made her entire body felt heavy. She swayed on her feet, and her staff slid from her sweating, bloody hands. She lifted her head and thought she was imagining a curious sight of Lanard on fire. Arrows whizzed by her, the shouts of battling men, the wailing of the wounded; it was deafening and horrible, and she never wanted to hear it again. She next heard a whistling sound and gasped when she felt another painful strike on her body. Disoriented, her head bowed, she saw an arrow lodged under her right shoulder. She fell to her knees with no strength to stand, her sight fading. From behind, she was gently lowered to the ground as the flaming bridge collapsed into the river behind her.

"Fe t'obion," she whispered, and was aware of no more.

***

Nidale arrived at the flaming bridge as it collapsed into the river, and the battle appeared to be winding down. Across the river, he saw a man lower Naria to the ground, and another come to their aid. He shook his head in disbelief. *She's supposed to be safe! What a cruel fate this is!* He ran along the riverbank to the shallower part of the river to cross, frantically struggling through the current of waist-deep water. A medic crouched next to Naria and spoke to Casden.

"When I remove the arrow, there will be much bleeding."

Casden nodded and took Naria's hand. He whispered loving words, and two more soldiers brought a litter to the scene. The medic pulled the arrow loose, and those watching the scene winced at the action. He immediately applied a thick bandage to the spurting wound.

"Look at her, the brave girl," a soldier said sorrowfully and patted Casden on the shoulder.

"I don't know if the arrow went into her lung, but keep this bandage pressed on the wound. When the bleeding slows, place her on the litter and bring her to lie with the others."

He rose and left to tend to more of the wounded. Nidale arrived breathlessly at the scene. "What others?" he asked.

"The other wounded plainsmen. Brave as any soldiers, I'd say," a soldier grimly answered.

Nidale brought his attention back to the man that gently cupped Naria's face and kissed her brow. When he was about to ask why he was kissing his daughter, he was astonished to see her necklace and rings on their hands.

"Help me place her on the litter," Casden said to the nearest man.

He carefully grasped under her shoulders while another took her legs, and they laid her on the litter. Nidale stepped forward and took hold of the foot end. Casden took one look at him and knew who he was.

***

"Times like this make me want to curse fate," Nidale grumbled as he paced around the medical tent, kicking a clump of grass.

Naria, Doonay, Aldren, Tholan, and Danarin—the very ones sent away for their safety — all lay wounded and unconscious, tended to by their families. The young corporal, named Casden, refused to leave Naria's side. *What a way to meet my son-in-law!*

He also learned about the young mage helping tend to Aldren. She captured the hearts of Aldren's family when she marched into the healer's tent after the battle and announced, "I'm Jezzine Dranesta, a mage, and I'm in love with your son. Any questions?"

Aldren had met his match. Nidale smiled at the recollection of that moment and was brought back to the present by his wife's voice.

"When did you marry our Naria?" Leeda asked and patted Naria's fevered forehead.

"Ten days ago," Casden replied and smiled at the memory of their wedding day.

Someone tapped the pole supporting the tent flap, and Jezzine's face appeared in the opening. "It was a beautiful wedding."

"You were there?" Leeda asked.

"Yes, madam, I stood with her," replied Jezzine.

"Why don't you tell me about it?" Leeda requested and patted the stool next to her.

"Well, we worked all morning on her hair...."

Casden never left Naria's side. He helped change her dressings, cool her feverish body, and get as much broth down her throat as he could manage. At night, he slept on a cot next to her in case she woke. The morning after the battle, when Naria convulsed and coughed blood, Casden prayed for the first time when he heard the healer's prognosis.

"She's a fighter, but she's lost a lot of blood, more than I've ever seen someone lose and survive," the healer said.

***

That night, Nidale and Leeda went to the tent to say good night to Casden, but stopped outside the flap when they saw him kneeling at Naria's cot, clutching her hand.

"I did something I've never done before, pretty one, and you'd be proud. I prayed. I prayed to whoever is listening to take me, instead of you, if a life is required. You can't die; too many people want you, and I need you. I long to see your sweet smiles, and frowns when Jezzine and Aldren tease you."

Nidale put a finger to his wife's lips, not wanting to interrupt the endearing one-way conversation.

"I remember the look in your eyes when we married; it's what I see when I close my eyes. I can't live without looking into your pretty eyes and seeing your sweet smile. I know I can't live without you telling me you love me. Don't leave, please don't leave."

***

Five days later, her eyelids fluttered. Sounds around her were faint, and she felt as if she were floating.

"That's it, pretty one, slowly," a familiar, calming voice said.

She waited for the disorientation to pass and smiled at the kind voice and handsome face above hers.

"That's what I've been missing," he said and placed a featherlight kiss on her lips.

"Thank the heavens!" her mother exclaimed from the tent entrance.

Her raspy voice uttered something unintelligible. Jezzine poked her face around the tent entrance.

"She wants water," Jezzine said and entered the tent to kneel on Naria's other side.

She gently lifted Naria's head so that Casden could put the water skin to her mouth. Leeda rushed from the tent to find Nidale.

"Better?" he asked.

"Yes," Naria said with a clearer voice.

"I reckon you wish to know all that's happened. You gave all of us a fright when we found you after the battle," he said.

Casden told her they weren't sure she would live after the battle. He told her of the arrow that had pierced her lung, causing her to cough copious amounts of blood and convulse. "We won the day. Your people are safe and free."

Nidale swept into the tent and saw his daughter awake. He closed his eyes and bowed his head. *Thank the Great One!* He drew Leeda close and they shared a tearful embrace. Naria reached for them with her uninjured arm, thrilled to see them. How long had she dreamed of this reunion?

"There will be time enough for that. You've earned your rest," assured Nidale.

Leeda burst into tears again. "Our brave girl!"

The memory of Doonay with an arrow lodged in his leg caused her eyes to widen in alarm. "Doonay!"

"Is well and hates his walking stick," Nidale said. "The others are recovering as well."

She saw Casden and Jezzine glance at each other. Casden shook his head. "Not now."

"There's more?" Naria asked, fearing the worst.

"Do you feel well enough to hear it?" Casden asked and took her hand. Jezzine took the other.

"Will the news improve with time?" Naria asked.

"I wish I could say yes," Casden replied.

"Bristan fell," Jezzine said and quickly wiped a falling tear.

"As did Lidorn," Casden said gently.

A sudden thunderstorm echoed Naria's wails of sorrow. All except Casden left the tent to let her mourn in private.

***

Later in the day, she felt well enough to sit and nibble small bites of bread. The death of Lidorn was a heavy sorrow. Did Marden feel his death? Did Castanya feel Bristan's death when her night cat form faded?

"The sadness will fade over time, Naria."

Her father's voice startled her from her musings. He was the only one in the tent with her. She sighed sadly and plucked the hem of her tunic.

"But it will always be in the corner of my heart. I'll visit their resting places when I'm well enough to walk."

"As you wish."

"Where are the others?" she asked.

"Going about the business of restoring our village. Your husband is with his men. The army prepares to ride to Talamos."

"The home of the governor?" she drawled, mimicking the prince's voice of disdain.

He chuckled. "Would it surprise you to know that it's less than a day's ride away?"

She scoffed in frustration and threw her bread aside. "To think we traveled back and forth across the whole wide lands when you were so close! Fate has surely been amusing itself at our expense!"

"Such sage words for one so young," he teased.

"Lidorn said it often."

"Danarin blames himself," he said.

"What could he possibly blame himself for?" she asked.

"When told that we were less than a day's ride away, he went into seclusion. He blames himself for the fateful trek across the continent that almost led to your deaths, his words."

"Pashah! None of us had any way of knowing where you were! He made the best decision he could! In the end, it was best, wasn't it? We came back with an army and won our lives back," Naria declared.

"And you brought back a husband as well. He's told us briefly of your courtship, but your mother and I eagerly await the story as you tell it."

"Yes, father," she said, blushing.

"You mistake my meaning. Casden's a fine young man, a courageous soldier, and loves you beyond reason. He left his home and family to fight for yours, and I couldn't ask for a better husband than that for you. It matters not that he isn't one of our people."

***

That night, Casden emerged from the tent with Naria in his arms. Her companions, parents, and Jezzine sitting around a fire cheered at her appearance.

"We've missed you at suppertime," Aldren said.

"Where's Danarin?" she asked.

Tholan, with a bandage around his neck, cleared his throat and spoke. "He left for Baranos three days ago."

"He said he left something behind and wanted it back," Aldren said with a shrug, his lips twitching in amusement.

"Rillorna!" the companions chorused.

"What's a rillorna?" Leeda asked.

***

Two weeks after the Battle of South Peak, Naria sat between the graves of Lidorn and Bristan. She arranged the flowers atop the soil and straightened the simple marker adorned with three horizontal lines. She smiled at the marker that said **The Wizard Bristan**.

"It's been two weeks since the battle, brothers. I wish so much that you were here. Lidorn, you and my father would get along famously. He teases me endlessly about going all the way to Rylanos to find a husband. He's using your staff; I hope you don't mind."

She looked back to the grove where Casden and Jezzine talked, allowing her to visit the grave alone.

"The army departs tomorrow for Talamos. Based on what the prisoners have said, the Regent predicts a swift departure of the governor. When the army returns to Rylanos, Casden will resign and return here to take up woodworking."

"This sling is dancing on my last nerve. Father says it may come off when I can hold my staff," she stated adjusted the sling that held her right arm.

She coughed and patted her chest. "My lung is still healing, but my heart will take longer, I'm afraid. Your passing has been the hardest part of all this. I'll never forget you, brothers. May your spirits be at peace."

She rose and looked out over the field of fresh graves, now named the Field of Swords. Out of the 800 Rylanos soldiers at the battle, 198 fell. 198 were too many, in her opinion, but she was grateful beyond words that Casden wasn't among the dead. She lingered at the graves a minute more and then left to join her husband and Jezzine.

"I heard you cough. Are you well?" Casden asked.

"Yes, my heart, I'm well. I grow stronger every day. Are you well?" she replied, poking him in the side.

He huffed dramatically. "You had an arrow in your chest, yet you ask me if I'm well? Not only do you grow stronger, but you also grow more vexing as well."

She let out a long-suffering sigh. "Well, I am my father's daughter."

"As your mother says, and it's a wonder that between you and your father, she hasn't run for the hills long before now," he pointed out.

She stepped closer to him and nudged his neck with her lips. "Well, if you decide to run for the hills, they're that way, and I insist you take me with you," she said and kissed softly along his jaw.

Jezzine made a gagging sound and disappeared with a pop.

"Hey, lovebirds!" shouted Aldren from the bridge. "Come quickly; a wagon approaches that you have to see!"

"Move quickly, he says, as if," Naria quipped.

When they arrived at the temporary bridge made of logs and large stones, they heard a loud, familiar voice.

"This is what you call taking care of yourself?" Rillorna demanded from the carriage seat.

Naria's heart thrilled at the sight of her. Danarin climbed from the seat and helped her down. The woman immediately went to Naria, and they shared a joyful reunion.

"Danarin told me all that's happened. Must you be so brave? I certainly want to know the man who captured that sweet heart of yours," she said, smiled at the man with an arm around her waist.

"Of course, but you must meet my parents as well. I'm so glad to see you. How long are you visiting?"

Rillorna chuckled. "For a long while, Danarin and I married four days ago."

"Danarin, you sly thing," Aldren teased.

***

That night, around a fire, Danarin and Aldren entertained the companions' families with tales of their journey. The night's highlight was Aldren's descriptive version of Naria's first and last experience with beer. The only one not laughing was Naria, who would be forever mortified that she had vomited on poor Danarin. Casden's arms were around her, holding her close.

"You're not angry, are you?" he asked, his lips tickling her ear.

"No, not really. It's good to hear everyone laugh, even if I'm the cause. Look, Father can hardly breathe from laughing so hard," she noted.

"It's getting late. Are you tired? Your voice sounds like it."

He stood and helped her to her feet.

"Good night to all of you," she said.

Her parents rose to embrace her, thanking the Great One for the miracle that was her life. The group laughed at her squeal when Casden swept her into his arms, and they continued to their tent.

To be continued in the next story. Thanks for reading!

Glossary

- **F'sana felia,** *falling leaf*

- **Pashah**! *Exclamation of surprised disbelief*

- **Hanoo,** *wild fowl, like a turkey*

- **Lankash!** *Swear word used in aggravation, not polite*

- **Larin root,** *bitter-tasting root used for sweets and medicine*

- **Taynot,** *coin of the highest value*

- **Ors'ghi** *horse, in the Old Language*

- **Wev'a** *woman, in the Old Language*

- **Mev'a** *man, in the Old Language*

- **Dultur** *sarcastically said 'dear one'*

- **Elif** *dirt, in the Old Language*

- **Sulin'ik** *bread, in the Old Language*

- **Ollen'ik** *meat, in the Old Language*

- **Jalic,** *cheap metal, like tin*

- **Quilium,** *expensive, best quality metal, like platinum*

- **An-end, stu** *Greetings friend, in the Old Language*

- **Admil, stu** *Good day friend, in the Old Language*

- **Porra bloom,** *calming flower used in medicine*

- **Caton devig fi paral?** *Do you understand Druidic?*

- **Lankash!** *curse, also not polite to use*

- **Turna!** *curse, not polite to use*

- **Jerna,** *coin of low value, like a penny*

- **Ranasta stone,** *amber-colored birthstone gem, fifth month*

- **Naria stone,** *bright green birthstone gem, sixth month*

- **Feen li ved feen li.** *He is what he is.*

- **Row-kosh,** *exclamation of appreciation, like whoa!*

- **Nial** *sky, in the Old Language*

- **Ba'nial,** *cloud, in the Old Language*

- **Ba'thon,** *rain, in the Old Language*

- **N'riss n'dar,** *Druidic chant to call the wind*

- **N'riss n'hav,** *Druidic chant to call the thunder*

- **N'ris n'thon,** *Druidic chant to call the rain*

- **N'riss iness,** *Druidic chant to call swirling water, cyclones*

- **N'riss n'bent,** *Druidic chant to lightning from the sky*

- **Fe t'obion,** *I'm home*

About the Author

Julie Naillon is a fifty-something veteran of the U.S. Marine Corps and U.S. Army. She calls Central Texas home where she lives with her husband of 27 years and has three children. She enjoys cooking, fishing, reading, movies, and is currently pursuing a graduate degree in English. She is a lifelong fan of sci-fi and fantasy genres, and this tale is her love letter in homage to the genres. Her must reads are *Lord of the Rings*, *The Dragonlance Chronicles*, and *The Wheel of Time*.